Lion People

MICHAEL MILONE

ARENA PRESS
NOVATO, CA

Copyright © 2010 Michael Milone

*For those who have been willing
to sacrifice their lives
that others might live in peace*

Chapter 1

Like so many recent hunts, this one had been more difficult than in times past. The people of the Wolf Clan had searched for the herd of mammoths for days. Some of the hunters wanted to give up and go home. The terrain was rugged, they were far from their village, and the weather was miserable and rainy. A few of them grumbled because the mammoth herds were becoming smaller than ever.

The animals they hunted were members of the elephant family. At the shoulder, they were more than twice the height of a grown man. They had a powerful trunk and long, curved tusks. These animals were able to withstand cold weather because of their fur and a thick layer of body fat. Like many other plant-eating animals, mammoths spent most of their time foraging for food.

"Look up on the ridge," said Tulio. "Griffo seems to have found the mammoths."

Without making a sound, the boy at the top of the ridge gestured to the other hunters. He had spotted the mammoths, and they should come to him. He did not shout for fear of scaring the great beasts.

The older men led the group, which included several boys, a girl, and two wolves. Maddia and her brother, Tulio, followed behind the others with the wolves, Nasha and Albo. Maddia had found Nasha, the gray wolf, as a pup. A year later, they had tamed Albo with the help of Nasha. Albo had somehow become separated from his pack and was wandering alone. The two wolves were now part of their clan, as were the puppies that had been born to them not long ago.

When they got to Griffo, the group was careful to speak quietly and remain hidden from the mammoths. They did not want to frighten the herd after working so hard to find them. The mammoths had been grazing in the valley and were now on their way toward an open, grassy plain.

"They are just leaving the valley," whispered Griffo. "And look at the last mammoth. It has been wounded, perhaps in a fight with another male."

The trailing mammoth in the herd was clearly injured. It was limping on one of its front legs where there was a gash. A second puncture wound was on its shoulder. These were probably caused by the tusks of another mammoth, possibly the dominant animal. Mammoths sometimes fought for the leadership of the herd, and wounds of this kind were not unknown. The mammoth's wounds would probably heal over time, but while they did, it was more likely to be attacked by a pack of wolves or a group of humans.

Baratho, the clan leader, described the plan. Maddia and Nasha, along with two of the men, would get between the injured mammoth and the rest of the herd. They would make a commotion and hope that the herd would continue moving out of the valley and that the lone mammoth would retreat backward. Once it was separated from the herd, the hunters could attack with spears and rocks thrown from the sides of the valley. This strategy had evolved over many years and was surprisingly effective. Although this group assault on the mammoth was dangerous, it was less risky than any other method the clan had developed.

"What about Albo and me?" asked Tulio. The boy, who was almost as big as most of the men, felt a little left out of the plan.

Baratho smiled and put his hand on the boy's shoulder. "I would like you and the white wolf to stay here to help where it is necessary. If anything goes wrong in trying to separate the mammoth from the herd, we will have to be rescued. You two must serve as our reserve and be ready to move instantly. We are all depending on you. If we are in trouble, you will have to distract the mammoth and give us an opportunity to escape."

The answer was satisfactory, at least to the boy. The white wolf would much rather have been involved in the action. While the others moved into position, Tulio and Albo waited in a place that gave them easy access to either group of hunters. Albo was so eager to join the pursuit that Tulio had to sit beside him with his arm around the wolf's neck. "Be patient, my friend," he said to the wolf. "Our time will come."

Maddia and Nasha, along with two hunters, came down from the ridge. They moved quietly from rock to rock in order to stay out of sight. When they reached the valley floor, they hid in a clump of bushes growing among some large boulders. Even the most alert animals would have trouble noticing them.

The rest of the hunters worked their way behind the mammoth. They found a spot where they could descend from the ridge quickly. Holding their position, they waited for the right time to attack.

Baratho gestured to Maddia and the others near the mouth of the valley, and they burst out of their hiding place. They made as much noise as they could, hoping that the herd of mammoths would move in one direction and the lagging animal in another. Nasha chased the fleeing herd for a short distance, but once Maddia was sure they were moving off, she called the wolf, which bounded to the girl's side. The mammoth turned and shuffled back into the valley.

The hunters on the ridge moved down swiftly. One after another, they came as near to the mammoth as they could and threw their spears, hoping to add to the mammoth's injuries. Zibio managed to get close enough to run his spear into the side of the mammoth. It proved to be serious, and the mammoth became wobbly on its feet.

As the mammoth stumbled, the hunters who had been with Maddia ran up and stabbed it with their spears. Maddia stayed back, as she had been told, and kept Nasha away from the action. The two of them would only have added to the confusion as the hunters tried to finish off the mammoth. They also had to be prepared if the other animals in the herd changed direction.

By now, the mammoth had rolled onto its side and was dying. The hunt had gone better than anyone could have wished for, and none of them had been hurt. The meat from the mammoth would feed their tribe for many days. The tusks, skin, bones, and other body parts would be used by the clan. Nothing of the mammoth would be wasted.

Nevertheless, all of the hunters had mixed feelings. The mammoth was a beautiful beast that did not threaten humans, and nothing was as imposing as a mammoth herd on the move. The people of the clan thought that all living things had a special place in nature, and they only killed for food or to protect their lives. After a successful hunt, they would give thanks for the food they received and show their respect for the animal that sustained them.

Baratho turned to signal Tulio to come down from the ridge. The boy and the wolf bounded down, happy to be with the others. Like Maddia, Tulio held Albo back from the activity near the mammoth.

All the hunters had used their spears to bring the mammoth down. The spears were now stuck in the mammoth, and it was too dangerous to try to retrieve them.

"Maddia, let me have your spear," said Baratho. He repeated his request to Tulio.

Knowing what he had in mind, they handed their spears to Baratho, who in turn, passed one to Zibio, the father of Maddia and Tulio. With the mammoth on the ground, they could drive the spears into the heart or lungs and end the animal's life.

The clan leader and his friend approached the mammoth carefully. Together, they lunged at it, driving their spears as deeply into the animal as they could. They turned and ran from the animal as it passed through its death throes to the stillness of its end.

When the mammoth stopped moving, the hunters advanced cautiously. One at a time, they pulled their spears from the lifeless body. They gathered around the animal and tapped the butt ends of their spears on the ground. As a group, all of them chanted the ancient words of celebration and gratitude to the mammoth for all it would offer them through its passing. They honored the spirit of the animal as it left this world.

Moving the parts of the animal back to camp was hard work and would take two days. The hunters would carry as much as they could back to camp today. Tomorrow, they would return with others from the clan and get the rest of the animal. Some of the flesh would be eaten by animals in the night. There was little they could do about that. They could post guards and make a fire, but the threat of enemies and animals made that unrealistic.

"Cut the biggest pieces of meat," Baratho told Tulio and Lakus, his younger brother. "Leave the skin attached, and try to avoid bones. We shall put the meat on spears so it can be carried by two people on their shoulders. The skin is stronger than the meat and will help to keep it on the spear."

Turning to Zibio and Griffo, he said, "Take the tusks first. They are very useful, and we should not leave them here tonight. If they prove to be too heavy to be brought all the way to camp, we can hide them on the way."

Baratho oversaw the butchering. Tulio and Lakus had been on many hunts. This was the first time they had been asked to remove the meat. The clan leader showed the boys where the best pieces of meat were. He demonstrated how to cut the meat so that a spear could be passed through the skin. This would allow two or more pieces of meat to be hung from a spear. A pair of hunters could then lug the meat on their shoulders.

"Maddia, I think the wolves deserve a treat," suggested Baratho. He hacked off two pieces of meat and handed them to the girl.

The wolves were standing a short distance from the mammoth. They were eager to dine on the carcass, but they were obedient to Maddia, who had told them to stay where they were. As she walked to them with the meat, they knew that it was for them. They wagged their tails in anticipation. When she gave the meat to them, they ate in distinctive ways that reflected their personalities.

Albo, the male, had been adopted as an older wolf. He took the meat at once, walked a few paces away, and ate it ravenously. Nasha had been raised from a pup by Maddia. She sniffed the meat, licked Maddia's hand, and took it gently. She looked at Maddia as if she would be willing to share the meat. Maddia petted her head and sat beside the wolf. Nasha understood that there was no need for her to share the meat, and she began eating.

When all was ready, Baratho led the group back to the village. He and Zibio started out in the lead. Each of them would alternate with one of the others who was bearing a heavy load, allowing the carrier to serve as the advance guard. By rotating the tasks, no one was overly burdened, and a fresh guard was always at the front of the group.

In the rear were Maddia, Tulio, and the wolves. They carried nothing because they had to control the wolves and be on the lookout for danger. The back of the group was the most likely place that an enemy or animal would attack. The wolves, because of their nature, would be able to detect a threat before the humans.

Fortunately, on this day, there was no danger. The group arrived at the camp late in the afternoon. Some of the meat was cooked for the feast that night. Extra meat would be used for the meals tomorrow. The remaining meat was impaled on spears outside of camp so animals would not get it. The meat would be cut into strips, dried, and smoked to preserve the meat for the future.

Everyone slept peacefully that night, content with a successful hunt. They were looking forward to the morning, when they would retrieve the rest of the mammoth. No one had any idea how eventful the next day would be.

Chapter 2

Three shadowy figures kneeled among the boulders at the side of the valley. They huddled together to stay warm because the morning air was cool. The sky was becoming brighter as evening slipped away.

When the sun rose above the hills that surrounded them, they looked carefully in every direction. Feeling confident they were safe, they trotted toward the slain mammoth on the ground in the middle of the valley. Using stone hand tools, they cut off pieces of meat and ate it raw. The three of them were near starvation and desperately needed food. Moreover, they knew that starting a fire might attract unwanted attention.

The woman and two girls worked quickly. After eating their fill, they took as much meat as they thought they could carry. The mammoth would provide them with food for several days.

They did not know when they would find meat again.

"Let me show you how to cut the skin," said Tali, the older of the girls. She slid her tool between the skin and the meat. They separated easily because her blade, made of the black stone called obsidian, had an unbelievably sharp edge. Tali cut the piece of hide off and then repeated the process two more times. These pieces of skin would let them carry the meat.

The woman worked silently, cutting strips of meat from the carcass. She looked at the pieces of skin that Tali held and smiled. Her daughter had not only learned well how to use the knife, but she was teaching her younger sister, Dani.

Unknown to the three of them, they were being watched. A cave lion had wandered over the ridge, attracted by the smell of mammoth. With barely noticeable steps, the huge beast crept stealthily down the slope. It was a short distance from the humans when the woman saw the lion.

The cave lion was a vicious predator. The largest of the big cats ever to walk the planet, it was a ruthless killing machine. Despite its size, this lion moved both quietly and swiftly. Few animals could defend themselves against a fully-grown cave lion, which struck out with a claw to disable the prey and kill it with a bite of its powerful jaws. Humans feared cave lions, but they often honored them in ceremonies, hoping that showing respect might move the spirit of the lions to spare them.

This lion, however, did not care if humans honored its kind. It was hungry and would have fed on the mammoth had the humans not been around. Their presence triggered its hunting instinct, and the lion crouched low to the ground.

The woman knew they were all in peril. The mammoth had meat enough for a dozen lions, but there was no way the three of them could leave without attracting its attention. She understood at once what she had to do. In order to save her children, she must lure the lion away and sacrifice her life.

Turning to the girls, she used a series of gestures, pointing out the lion, silencing them, and signaling that she would move off. They must go in the other direction, and she pointed toward a small opening among several rocks. If the girls could make it to the crevice, the lion might not be able to get to them.

Despite knowing her fate, the woman did not give in to her urge to hug the girls. She touched each of the girls, not wanting to distress them further with a tearful hug. She took a deep breath and turned to confront the lion.

Vica walked away from the girls. She chanted in a low voice, making one of the few sounds she could hear. The chant was something she had learned as a girl, for although she could not hear the voices of other humans, she could feel the vibrations of her own voice. These sounds could be heard by others, and they were often made during the ceremonies of her clan. Her people were convinced that Vica had a special gift and could sense their prayers despite being unable to hear their voices. She was also aware of the sound of the drum and could chant in time with the other members of her clan.

The chant brought Vica some measure of peace. She knew that the lion would take her life, and she prayed that her journey to the spirit world would be swift and painless. Her chant, combined with the belief that she had saved her daughters, let her enter a trance-like state. She turned to look at the lion, which had followed her with its eyes in preparation for an attack.

Tali and Dani had done what their mother had indicated. They moved to the rocks and crawled as far inside as they could. They brought the meat they had cut from the mammoth, as their mother had told them. Tali gave the meat to Dani and positioned herself protectively in front of her sister. As quietly as she could, Dani moved small rocks to the block the opening. They were as safe as they could be, given the circumstances.

Seeing that the girls had made it to the cleft in the rocks, Vica was about to run in order to draw the lion from them. But for some reason unknown to Vica, the lion had looked away. Standing up from its crouch, the lion began moving up the slope again, glaring into the distance occasionally. Vica could was bewildered by what was happening. For a moment, her heart was filled with hope. Then she looked in the direction of the lion's gaze.

The cause of the lion's retreat was obvious. Two wolves were approaching, and the rest of the pack was probably not far behind. A cave lion might survive a battle with a pack of wolves, but it might not. This lion pranced off, perhaps to return to the mammoth at a later time.

As quickly as Vica's hopes had been raised, they were dashed. The wolves were a more serious threat than the lion. A pack of wolves would make short work of her, and because they can smell better than the lion, they would detect the scent of the girls. Being somewhat smaller than the lion, the wolves might be able to work their way into the gap and get to the girls.

Vica turned and pulled the cutting stone from her tunic. She would have given her life to the lion without a struggle, but not the wolves. She may be able to injure one or more of the wolves before they killed her, which increased the chances of her daughters' survival.

The wolves trotted toward her at a slower pace than Vica expected, and the rest of the pack did not appear. In fact, as the wolves drew near, they stopped running and walked cautiously. As if on command, they halted, and to her amazement they sat still not ten paces from her. What was more astounding was that several humans ran from the rocks toward her and the wolves, and the animals seemed to be waiting for them.

The lead person in the group seemed to be no more than a boy. He ran toward her shouting in a way that was not threatening. Being deaf, she could not hear him, but his face showed a mix of concern and reassurance. She interpreted his look correctly, for Griffo had seen the lion prepare for its assault. He was relieved that it had chosen to withdraw rather than to challenge the wolves.

"Are you all right?" he asked as he came to Vica. He gestured at the others, who stayed with the wolves. Although the wolves were comfortable with humans, Griffo was aware that most people they encountered regarded the wolves as a threat. Considering what the woman had just been through, he did not want to add to her distress.

Vica responded by moving her head up and down. She could not hear his words, but she knew what he had asked from his expression, the shaping of his lips, and the situation. She was relieved and replaced her cutting tool in her tunic. She held out her hands with her palms up, a gesture that was universally recognized as a greeting. There was no weapon in her hand, and her fists were unclenched.

Pointing toward the wolves, Vica made a gesture that suggested she did not understand. Griffo knew what she was wondering, having gone through the same experience with others who did not know the story of how his clan had tamed the wolves.

"Do not be afraid," the boy said shaking his head. "They are not dangerous. They are our docgas." He spoke the word the people in the region used for the wolves who lived with them. The word "docga" described a stranger who came to humans at a time of great need to help them through the difficulty. Docgas might stay with the clan or disappear just as mysteriously as they had arrived. The wolves were, indeed, docgas, and they had been of service to the clan in many ways.

The woman pointed at her ears and put her hands over them. She wanted him to understand that she could not hear. She then motioned to him, encouraging him to come with her. She led him to a small opening among the rocks, bent over, and waved. Some of the rocks were dislodged, and to the boy's surprise, two girls crawled out. They held pieces of meat in skins, which they clutched tightly to their chests.

The taller girl strode up to him while the younger one clung to the woman's leg. "Mother cannot hear," she said. "Nor can she speak. She understands many things, and she uses hand movements with us. Do not think she is stupid, as some people have. She is the bravest and wisest woman I have ever known. I am Tali, my sister is Dani, and our mother is Vica."

Griffo smiled at Tali and bowed to the girl as a sign of respect and understanding. He held his hand out to the girls and Vica in friendship. The boy knew at once that the woman and the girls must be very capable indeed to have survived on their own this far from any settlement.

"I am called Griffo. We killed this mammoth yesterday. I see you have taken some of the meat, to which you are welcome. There is plenty for us all. Do not be frightened by us or the wolves. I will tell you their story."

As Griffo spoke, he saw that the girl moved her hands. Vica's eyes dodged back and forth between Griffo and Tali's hands. She nodded to show that she understood. The kindness of the boy was evident, and she showed no anxiety when he waved his hand and the rest of the group approached with the wolves.

The girls slid behind their mother as the other humans and wolves got closer. The wolves sniffed the woman and the girls, who despite their fear of the animals, could not resist holding out their hands to let the wolves smell them.

"The gray one is Nasha, and the white one is Albo," said the girl who had followed Griffo. "My name is Maddia. You look hungry."

Maddia pulled out some seed cake out of her tunic. She broke it into pieces and gave it to Tali and Dani, who ate it eagerly. Smiling, she pulled the arm of the boy who was behind her. She reached into a fold of her brother's tunic and took out another seed cake, which she handed to Vica. "Tulio is my brother, and there has never been a time when he did not have extra food."

To Maddia's surprise, Vica seemed to understand everything she said, even though neither Dani nor Tali had gestured. She had heard the girl tell Griffo that her mother was not stupid, and now she knew exactly what Dani meant. Her mother could not hear or speak, but her mind was as sharp as anyone's. She understood from Maddia's behavior that she was teasing her brother.

A dozen more people joined them, most of whom were men, but a few women were with them. There was much talk among them as Griffo explained what he knew of the woman and the girls. In time, they would return to their village with the rest of the mammoth. The three strangers would be invited to go with them. For the moment, however, they relaxed with the woman and girls to give them time to recover from the ordeal.

Chapter 3

On the trip back to the camp, the going was slow because they had to carry the meat, skin, and bones of the mammoth. They took rest breaks often throughout the day. During the walk, Vica, Tali, and Dani learned about the people who rescued them and told them about themselves.

The girls were very interested in how the wolves came to be with the clan. Maddia discussed how she had found Nasha as an abandoned pup in a cave, had fed her, and had eventually brought her to camp. Tulio and Katia told about how Maddia and Nasha had chanced upon Albo and how he had come to the clan. Tali and Dani could hardly believe the stories, but the proof was here. They could not wait to get to camp, where the others had told them that there were more wolves, the pups of Nasha and Albo.

"And where did you come from?" Maddia asked Tali.

"What do you mean?" responded the girl.

"Before we found you, where had you been?"

Tali looked at her mother, who gestured so the girl knew she could tell the story. "We were prisoners of a powerful clan. We did the gathering for them and worked around the camp like slaves. They moved every few years. They would attack a village, kill the men, and steal what they could. They would capture the women and children. That is how mother ended up with them. If the clan was large, they might take over the whole village and make it their home."

"We escaped many days ago. We have been wandering from place to place. Mother does not know this area or the clans who live here. Because we did not know who was friendly with our captors, we did not make contact with any of the clans. We wanted to get far away and hoped a clan would accept us."

"When were you captured?" asked Maddia.

"We were not captured," said Tali. "We were born in a camp. That is what mother said. We moved from camp to camp with our captors. I can only recall two camps. We fled from one of them."

After walking for a time, they stopped briefly to rest. When they resumed, Maddia, Tulio, and the two wolves walked at the rear with Fong, the toolmaker of the clan.

"Life has been harsh for the three of them," said Maddia. "I cannot imagine what it must be like to be a captive for so long."

Tulio added, "I wonder if they will want to stay with us. What do you think, Fong?"

"Only time will tell if they will stay. They will certainly be welcome. When I came to the clan, Ushga was the leader. He took me in with his family, but others offered their homes to me as well. When Griffo lost his parents, Leeza took him in immediately, despite the fact that her mate had died and she already had two children. I would be happy to let Vica and the girls stay with me."

Fong continued, "Which clan are they are talking about? There are not many clans who are warlike as the one they describe."

"What clan do you think they were with?" asked Maddia.

"I do not really know," answered Fong. "We have been dawdling while we talked. Let us catch up with the others," and he hurried them along. He did not wish to discuss his thoughts with the young people, hoping that what he was thinking was not true.

Later in the afternoon, they came to a place where several trails merged. Baratho told everyone to rest again while he and Tulio went to the river. They expected to find traders there. Two streams flowed into the river nearby, and it widened as it made a big bend. Traders sometimes assembled there because the trails passed near the river. Some of them even traveled on the river in dugout canoes.

From a distance, they saw people by the river.

Some of them jumped up and assumed a defensive pose when they the two humans and a wolf appeared. One who had remained seated stood up and spoke with the others, who then relaxed a little. He walked forward to greet them.

"Baratho, I have not seen you since last spring. If my memory is correct, you are Tulio. Forgive me, but I have forgotten the name of the wolf."

"It is good to see you, Valtar. The wolf is Albo. I am surprised that you remember Tulio, he has grown so much."

"I am honored that you remembered me," said Tulio. "I am also grateful that you were willing to help us." Tulio referred to an incident in which Valtar and his men were involved. They were part of the group that saved the pups of Nasha and Albo from being kidnapped by Gortush and Jartush.

Albo, who had become accustomed to new humans, sniffed Valtar, who gave him a small piece of dried meat before petting him. The wolf lay down by Valtar's feet and chewed on the meat.

"I am still mystified by what you have done with the wolves. How are the pups?" Valtar asked.

"Much bigger and more enthusiastic," said Tulio. "When the next litter comes, we hope you will accept at least one into your clan."

"We would welcome a wolf, but you will have to teach us what to do. My children often ask me to retell the story of Maddia and the wolf. Perhaps one day they can visit our village."

"So what do you have to trade today?" asked Baratho. "We have much of a mammoth not far from here."

"We have some dried fish, skins from antelope goats, and olives. The traders from the River Clan are here, and they will have other things."

While Baratho and Valtar discussed the terms of the trade, Tulio and Albo ran back to where the others were resting. The boy had some of them follow him back to the river, and the remainder went on to the settlement. When they arrived, they were surprised to see their leader eating olives and enjoying them.

Although humans had been eating olives for thousands of years, they did so only when they were near starvation. The fruit of the olive tree was nutritious and filling, but it tasted terrible. Olives have a very bitter flavor.

"Has Valtar persuaded you that olives are tasty?" asked Lakus, one of the group that carried the parts of the mammoth to the river.

"You will not believe what he told me, but first you must taste these."

With that, Baratho exchanged two pieces of the mammoth for an animal skin filled with olives in a liquid. Lakus and Tulio each tasted an olive tentatively. Seeing that their friends did not grimace, Griffo and Piero tried them.

"What did you do to remove the bitterness?" asked Piero as he reached for another.

Valtar told the tale he had heard. "One of the

clans near the salty sea has been trading these olives. Their clan has a story about the discovery, but I do not know if it is true. Many years ago, during a fall storm, some olive trees were blown from a cliff to a rocky beach below. The trees with their fruit were lodged in the rocks, so the olives were in the salty water. Some foragers had been stranded in a cave by the storm for several days and were overcome with hunger. When the storm abated, they immediately went to the beach to hunt for fish and shellfish. They found the olive trees as well, and because they were so hungry, ate the bitter fruit. They found out that the olives that had been soaked in salt water were much less bitter. After that, they started storing olives in salty water."

"The story is reasonable," said Baratho, "but truthfully, I do not care. The cured olives are much better than the raw ones I have eaten, and from now on, we will put olives for a time in salt water before eating them."

While the others were completing the trade, Piero looked down the river. What he saw he could not comprehend. A boy seemed to be standing on the surface of the water holding a pole.

"How is that boy walking on water?" he asked.

"He is not walking on water," answered Valtar. "He is standing on a raft made of logs tied together with vines."

Piero and his friends could not resist. They

rushed down the bank of the river to get a good look. They passed some people making dugout canoes by carving or burning the insides of logs. They had heard of these and had seen a few on the river. The dugout canoes were a way to use the river to travel. Their clan had little use for such vessels because the stream near their camp was too small.

When they climbed a slight hill beside the river, they got a good look at the boy and the raft. He was pushing the raft with a long pole and was heading to the other side of the river. They saw how the raft consisted of more than ten logs tied together. Two larger logs were tied underneath them for added stability. The buoyancy of the logs kept the boy above the water. He was too far away to speak to, but some people were below them near the water. They rushed down to talk to them.

"Do you know the boy with the raft?" asked Piero.

"Yes," said a woman, "he is my son. He just brought us across the river."

"Did he bring people and goods across the river?" said Griffo with an incredulous voice.

"He does that almost every day," said the woman proudly. "He built the raft himself. He learned how from the people of the sea. They were surprised that we did not know of the raft. We had always walked across the river down below where it is shallow. The crossing was risky at best, and when there is rain, it is impossible."

They watched as the boy drew up to the far bank. Another person got on the raft with what looked like a small animal. The boy pushed the raft off with the pole and floated across the river. The passenger got off carrying a small wild pig that had been roasted.

"Arik," said the woman, "these boys have been admiring your raft."

The boy stepped off the raft and pulled it onto the bank. He put the pole down carefully so it was out of the way and would not float off. He smiled, grateful for the attention.

"Was it hard to make?" asked Tulio.

"Not really. I had assistance cutting the wood. A man from one of the sea clans showed me how to tie the logs together. He came to our clan to trade and saw how challenging it was to cross the river. He said the raft would make the trip easier. Now I do this every day. People give me food, shells, and other things to ferry them back and forth."

While Arik talked about the raft, Piero examined it closely. He noted how the logs were tied together and to the crossways logs underneath.

"Why do the logs have cuts in them?" he asked Arik.

"The logs can rub against the vines and cut them through. When they are in the grooves, they are not rubbed as much. The grooves also keep the vines from sliding off the log. This can happen sometimes when the water is blown by the wind or the current is strong."

"Can you take me across the river and back?" begged Piero. He thought briefly and said, "In exchange, I can give you a piece of twine made from the hair of a wolf." He unwrapped one piece of the twine that he had tied around his waist to hold his tunic in place. Piero carried several pieces of this twine this way because it was so useful.

Arik looked at the twine carefully and felt it with his fingers. He had never seen a piece of twine like this, and he could tell from the feel that it was from a wolf.

"Let us go," he said smiling. "Do any of you want to come along?"

Although the others wanted to join them, they did not. If there was a problem, Tulio wanted to be ready in case he had to swim to rescue Piero, who could not yet swim. Lakus and Griffo felt responsible to stay on the bank to protect Baratho if it became necessary. There was no immediate threat of danger, but they were concerned because of the story told by Tali.

Arik picked up the pole and pushed the raft into the river. He held it stable so Piero could get on it. He sat on the edge of the raft, pushed away with the pole, and then used the pole to stand up. With strong pushes, he moved the raft easily across the river. Piero, who had been sitting, stood up and tried to balance himself on the raft.

After watching Arik for a time, Piero asked, "May I try it?"

Arik handed the pole to Piero, who pushed in the same way that his new friend had. His strokes were unsteady, and both of them almost fell into the water. Piero quickly got the hang of it, however, and they made it to the other bank. Arik described how to make a last push with the pole to get the raft on the bank, jumping off, and pulling the raft farther onto the shore.

For the return trip, Piero learned how to push the raft from the bank to the river. He used the pole handily, and their crossing was uneventful. When he brought the raft to the bank, his friends cheered his new talent. They had no idea if it would ultimately be useful, but knowing about the raft seemed to be one of those things that might come in handy.

"Our business is done," said Baratho, who had walked to them. "Now you have another opportunity to show how strong you are. The goods for which we traded are with Valtar. Let us take them back to our village. I think you will be received well because of the olives, and I am certain that Piero will have much to tell everyone about his adventure on the raft."

Chapter 4

When the group reached the camp, the rest of the clan greeted them. Among the most loving reunions were between the wolves and their pups. The strangers were completely unprepared for the joy conveyed by the pups and were amazed by the way they related to the humans.

Vica, Tali, and Dani were uneasy when they initially entered the camp, expecting to be outsiders in an event meant for family and friends. They were surprised, however, when they became the center of focus. They were welcomed in a way they had never experienced, and the attention was almost overwhelming. Several families volunteered at once to take them into their homes.

"They must spend the night with us," said Lura, one of the women who had been on the hunt. "My father and I have a large shelter, and it has been lonely since the passing of my mother." Turning to Vica, she added, "You have no obligation to stay with us, but we want you to be comfortable on your first night."

Hearing her daughter's suggestion, her father walked over to the newcomers. "My name is Alek, and I am Lura's father. I would be honored if you would stay with us."

Tali and Dani looked at their mother, who could think of nothing to say. The acts of kindness they had been given this day were unimaginable. Vica struggled to show her gratitude, and seeing this, Lura said, "Come, let us look at the shelter," and both she and her father shepherded Vica and the girls to their home.

While they walked, Dani and Tali looked around at what they hoped would be their new home. Boys and girls their age walked with them, smiling and chatting. They had never seen anything like this in their camp, where fear was the most common emotion.

At the shelter, Alek pulled back the cover from the opening and ushered the women and girls in. The hut was roomy, with animal skins on the ground around a central cooking fire. A smoke hole was in the roof, and baskets were here and there. To the girls, it was the most wonderful place they had ever seen. Best of all, it might be their home.

"This will be your sleeping area," said Alek, and he unfolded some animal skins on the side of the shelter that butted against a cliff. "And do not be concerned if one of the wolves snuggles up

Return of the Lion People

with you at night. He is with the other wolves now, but I am sure he will be back shortly."

The girls sat on the skins, and although it was not yet cool, they wrapped them around their shoulders. On many nights in other places, they had nothing to keep them warm other than the clothes they were wearing.

As if he heard his name being called, a young wolf bounded through the opening and into the shelter. He pushed his head into Lura's hand, demanding to be petted. He did the same with Alek before turning to the visitors. He sniffed Vica and then circled to the girls, who were a little frightened until he licked their faces and flopped down on them.

By now, tears were streaming down Vica's face, but she made not a sound. She had never seen her daughters so happy. She turned so the girls would not see her tears and smiled at Alek and Vica. She grasped their hands in an expression of thanks that could not be misunderstood.

As the sun began to set, the clan met by the great fire. Pieces of meat from the mammoth were already roasting on sticks beside the fire. Belia and Murra formed small cakes made of ground seeds. They placed them on rocks in the fire. The rocks were hot, so the seed cakes baked quickly. In addition to the meat and seed cakes, fruit and nuts were piled on leaves by the fire.

"We do this after a successful hunt," said Lura

to Vica. "Tonight is also noteworthy because you and the girls are with us."

Tali and Dani stared at the group. The entire clan, from the youngest to the oldest, sat around the fire. With them were the two adult wolves and five younger ones. It was a scene they could not have imagined. Maddia steered the girls away from their mother to a group of young people. Her brothers, Tulio and Lakus, beat out a rhythm on drums made with animal skin stretched over a hollowed-out log. The others with them sang chants in time to the drumbeat.

"Did they make music where you were before?" asked Madia. She tapped her spear on the ground to match the drums.

"We had no music in the camp," answered Tali.

"Tell them about the flute," said Dani.

"When we gathered food, we were sometimes far from the guards. We made music with this." Dani pulled a small object from within her tunic. It hung from a strip of animal hide tied around her neck.

"This is a flute," she said. "It is made from the bone of a bird. A friend made it for us. It has holes, and you blow into it." As she spoke she showed them the flute, pointing out the place where she blew into it and the other holes. She explained that she would put her fingers over the holes to change the sound.

Tali brought the flute to her mouth and blew into it gently. The sound was too faint to hear well.

Lakus and Tulio ceased their drumming, and everyone else was silent. Thinking she had done something wrong, Tali stopped.

"Go on," said Maddia. "Let us hear the music from the flute. It seems mysterious."

This time, Tali blew a little harder. The flute could make only a few notes, but they were beautiful. The sound was like that made by a bird, yet more haunting. The music floated through the air and seemed to touch each person in a peculiar way. Until this moment, no one in the clan had heard anything like it coming from another human.

When Tali finished, all the young people clustered around her. They passed the flute from one person to another. Each of them handled it with reverence. To them, the flute was magical. When it came to Tulio, he looked it over carefully.

"Fong and I can make other flutes," he said, and he handed it back to Tali. "But none will be as special as yours. You have brought us a new kind of music. We would be grateful if you would teach us to play."

The group was quiet for a moment. The stillness was broken by Lakus, who caused much laughter when he said, "May we eat now?"

As they ate, Maddia asked Lartha a question. "Why did we not know about making a flute? Is it not something we should have discovered ourselves? Why did none of the other clans tell us about this way of making music?"

"I have thought about the same thing," she said.

"So did I," added Baratho. He had overheard Maddia's question to Lartha and sat down to join them.

"Think about when Leeza learned how to make baskets." Baratho continued. "The clans who traded with us were amazed. Valtar told me that the people in his clan asked him why they had not discovered it. I guess the answer is that different groups of humans have discovered different things."

"But we told others about Leeza's baskets," said Maddia. "No one told us about the flute."

"None of the clans that are near us or who trade with us probably knew about making music this way," said Lartha. "The people who were captives with Vica most likely came from other places. Think about the people who have seen the wolves. They cannot believe that wolves and humans live together."

"That is different," suggested Griffo, who had joined the conversation. "Maddia found Nasha by accident. Inventions like the flute did not happen by accident."

By now, other people had crowded around the four of them. They wanted to hear what Baratho and Lartha had to say about the flute and other discoveries.

"Many of our original ideas have been unintended," said Belia. "When Lakus got Nasha's fur on his hands, he rubbed them together. The fur stuck together, and from that, we learned how to make twine from the fur of our wolves."

"The same was true of Leeza's bowls," said Fong. "We put soft clay figures in the fire, and they became solid. From this accident, she thought of making bowls of clay and baking them. Now we have bowls that can hold liquids as well as other things."

"There is one other notion to consider," said Lartha. "Stories from long ago say that there were fewer humans then. Our people lived apart from one another. If a person in one tribe had a good idea, it might never reach another tribe that was far away. Over time, the number of humans increased. There are more humans now than before. All of the clans have more people. Some of the people split off from their clans and travel to other places. They start new clans. They bring with them the innovations of their old clan. And there is more trading between the clans."

"Think of our story," said Baratho. "We were forced away from our village by the sea because of the action of Jartush and Gortush. We had to travel with only the things we could carry and the ideas we knew. Luckily, we found this valley, and things went well for us. Now we have a herd of aurochs in the canyon. Leeza has invented the basket and the bowl. Tulio learned to throw a spear. We have shared our knowledge with the neighboring clans. They shared their knowledge with us and let us hunt near them."

"I think I understand," thought Griffo out loud. "Because there are more humans, we devise more things. We encounter other humans more often, and we share our ideas through trade and friendship. It is almost as if we make one another smarter."

"Even the animals make us smarter," said Maddia. "Remember how Nasha taught us to swim?" For the benefit of Tali and Dani, she retold the story of how Katia had learned to swim by watching Nasha, and then Maddia and Tulio learned. Now, many of the young people of the clan could swim.

"But not the old people," added Lakus, and once again, everyone chuckled at the boy's words. He was, however, correct. Not one of the adults in the clan had learned to swim.

The hooting of an owl in the distance interrupted the conversation. Maddia turned to Dani and Tali and asked, "Do you know any owl stories?"

The owl was special to the Wolf Clan and other tribes. Some people feared owls, while others thought they were exceptional creatures that helped humans. On some nights Maddia and her friends would go just outside the perimeter of the camp. They would listen to the owls hooting back and forth to one another. Their sound was like people talking. Lartha said that owls carried the spirits of humans who had died to the other place, so owls deserved to be honored.

Dani smiled and said, "The owl has been our friend. When we made our escape, the owls shared the night with us. Their sounds reassured us, and when they were silent, we knew that hunting animals or humans were nearby, so we could hide."

Vica watched her daughters talking to her new friends. Although she could not hear what they said, she knew that the girls were as carefree as they had ever been. She hoped that bonding with the Wolf Clan would erase the memories of the years they had spent as captives. In the back of her mind, however, she still worried that the heartless clan that had imprisoned them and so many others would eventually find them.

Chapter 5

Like other groups of humans, the Wolf Clan cooked their meat by roasting over a fire. The simplest way this was done was to put a piece of meat on a stick and hold it in a fire. Large pieces of meat could be put on a strong stick. The stick and meat could be supported by other sticks over the fire. Sometimes the stick was held in place by rocks.

One night, as they sat around the fire in the middle of the village, Tali wrapped some meat, mushrooms, and figs in leaves. She pushed it into the edge of the fire and put a stone on top of it.

"What are you doing?" asked Lakus. "Do you not want your food? I will be happy to eat it."

"I am cooking the meat together with the other things," said Dani. "Do you not prepare food that way?"

"Sometimes we do," said Leeza, one of the women. "Lakus does not pay much attention to how we make the food. He is more interested in eating it. Where did you learn about cooking food in leaves?"

"When we were captives," she answered. "We did not have much food. Some of the food tasted awful and was hard for us to chew. One of the people with us came from beyond the salty sea. She showed us how to wrap food in leaves and put it in the fire. Cooking this way made the food softer and taste better."

"How long must it stay in the fire?" asked Lakus.

Maddia and the others rolled their eyes. Knowing Lakus, they realized that he wanted to taste what Dani was preparing. No one in the clan liked food more than Lakus, including his brother, Tulio, another hearty eater. Although he was young, Lakus was tall and strong, and he seemed to need a lot of food.

"Different foods require different times. Roots take the longest. Sometimes we would place meat, roots, and other plant parts near the fire overnight. We could eat them in the morning. The food I am making tonight will not take long. The meat was already roasted, and the mushrooms and figs cook quickly?"

"Can I try it now?" asked Lakus.

Everyone chuckled at the boy. In a friendly way, Leeza said, "Dani will tell us when it is cooked. For now, eat the seed cake you have in your hand. This will make it a little tastier.

Leeza put a piece of meat on the seed cake that Lakus held. She folded it in half so her nephew would be able to handle it more easily. He looked at the odd thing that Leeza had done, shrugged his shoulders, and gobbled it down. Tulio thought it looked good, so he did it, too.

The young people asked Tali and Dani more questions about their captivity. They were saddened to hear how difficult life was for them. Life was not easy for anyone in those days, but what the girls had gone through seemed especially harsh.

"Did you have any fun at all?" asked Maddia.

"We made little figures out of clay," said Dani. "People from different clans had games. We would make pictures on the walls of the cave with burnt sticks. Sometimes we would carve in the walls with rocks."

Tulio asked, "What did you draw? We also draw on the walls of caves. Maybe you can go with us to the story cave."

"We drew mostly animals," answered Dani, "and the sisters in the sky."

"Who are the sisters?" asked Katia.

"In the night sky, there are six stars together. We call them the sisters."

"So do we," said Maddia. "In our story, they are sisters who loved to dance around the fire. They danced so beautifully that the Great Spirit let them rise into the sky so that all could see them."

"That is a beautiful story," said Dani. "Our story

was different. The sisters were once held captive, too. They broke free and went into the sky. When we looked at them, we dreamed that one day we could get away."

"And you did," said Lura. "You two and your mother outsmarted your captors. The sisters gave you strength. Some day all those who are being held will be free."

The girls became quiet at the thought of their friends who were still prisoners. Their mood was quickly changed by Lakus, who said, "Do you think the food in the leaves is done yet?"

Dani used a stick to move the leaves from the fire to a flat rock. She carefully opened up the leaves. With another small stick, she speared a mushroom and handed it to Lakus. He nibbled at it and smiled.

"This is wonderful. It tastes like a mushroom, but is a little softer than usual. There are some other flavors mixed in with it. I can taste the juice from the meat and the fig."

The others all tasted what Dani had made. In a moment, it was gone, and she had not gotten any. She did not seem to care and was pleased that they liked what she had prepared.

"You were so kind that you got nothing yourself," said Leeza. "Here, we can make more, and this time, I will make certain that you get some."

With the help of Leeza and Belia, Maddia's mother, all of the young people cooked food in leaves. They made a mess, and much of the food was dropped in the fire, but they had fun doing it. Belia had a thought about a different way of cooking, but she did not mention it that night.

In the morning, Belia dropped by her sister's hut. "Leeza, while we were cooking with leaves last night, something came to mind. We have cooked with leaves before, but it can be messy. We can only make a little bit of food at a time. The food tastes good, however. What if we cooked the food in one of your bowls? That would be less messy, and we could prepare more of it at one time."

The bowls that Belia was talking about were made from clay. Leeza had accidentally found that clay bowls hardened when they were put in a fire. Now they made the bowls to hold things, including water.

"We can try," said Leeza. "Let us do it with the midday meal. We do not know how long it will take for the food to cook."

Leeza chose a bowl that was fairly wide and heavy. She thought that a strong bowl would be less likely to break. They looked at the different foods they had that might go well together. There was some meat left over from the night before, some mushrooms, some leafy greens, and some root vegetables.

"Do you think we should cut the food before cooking it?" asked Belia.

"Probably. Smaller things cook faster than

larger things. And I think we should add some water."

"Do you have any salt?" asked Belia.

"A little," said her sister. "I am glad you thought of that. Many people seem to like a little salt with their food."

Salt was precious to the clan and other people. Long ago, when they lived by the sea, they had plenty of it. Now they had to trade for it. They also found some salt near some small lakes in the area, but the nearest one was more than a day's walk distant. They liked the flavor that salt gave to food, and they found that salting food allowed it to last longer without spoiling.

The two of them cut the food and put it in the bowl with water and a little salt. Belia added a wood to the cooking fire. When they went to put the bowl on the fire, they found that it did not work very well. The bowl kept the fire from burning well at first. They became concerned that when the fire got hotter, it might cause the bowl to break. This had happened with some of the clay pieces that Leeza had baked in Fong's hearth.

"Put some stones by the fire," said a voice. "Then arrange the bowl on the stones so it is almost over the fire."

Tulio, Belia's older son, came into the shelter as he spoke. He had been looking for Belia, and his father had told him where she was.

"Fong and I had the same problem when we were baking clay shapes or trying to melt stones.

We could not control the heat of the fire very well. We discovered that moving objects around the fire let us avoid damaging what we were heating."

"So we can increase or decrease the heat by moving the bowl closer to or farther from the fire?" asked Belia.

"I think so," continued Tulio. "You can watch the food cooking. If it starts to smoke or boil, you can move it. And be sure to push it with a stick. If you grab the pot with your hands, you will be very unhappy. I have done that several times."

"So why were you looking for me?" asked Belia.

"I wanted to talk to you about the olives," replied Tulio. "Everyone loved the olives in salty water. Do you think we can make some ourselves? I do not know if we will be able to trade for them in the future."

"Be sure to save the salty water when all the olives are eaten. We can use that to cure more olives," suggested Leeza.

"We can get more salt from the dry lake," added Tulio. "We can make our own salty water for the olives. If we pick enough olives in the fall, we will be able to trade them." He looked at some of the bowls in Leeza's shelter. "Leeza, your bowls would be perfect for curing olives. When you make another batch of bowls, I can assist you. We can make a sizable one together. The only worry will be getting a fire big enough to bake it. Fong can probably be of service to us." Pausing for a moment, he said, "The food you are cooking smells wonderful."

"It will not be ready for a while," said Leeza. "Come back for the midday meal. And hope that our cooking tastes as good as it smells."

When the sun was high, Tulio returned. Maddia, Lakus, and the wolves were with him. From outside the shelter, Nasha and Albo smelled the food cooking. They paced around the shelter but did not go in. Their arrival was far from stealthy, and the women heard them.

"We will come out," said Belia. "There is not enough room for all of us and the wolves, and I know they will not wait quietly beside the shelter."

Leeza came out carrying the bowl of cooked food. She and Belia had removed it from the fire earlier in order to let it cool. It was warm and smelled delicious. The wolves were tempted by it, but Maddia make them sit a little distance away.

"We have an interesting complication," said Belia. "It is something we never thought about before. Normally when we eat, we use our fingers. We can easily eat seed cakes, meat, fruit, and vegetables this way. When we cook the food in a bowl, it becomes softer. There is no easy way to pick it up and eat it."

"Can we not eat it as we generally do?" asked Lakus. "I am willing to pick up the food from the bowl with my fingers."

Belia tapped her youngest child on the head

and smiled. "Of course you would. I suspect that you could eat everything we cooked, but there has to be a way to do it that is less messy. If we all reached into the bowl at once, it would be even harder to get the food out."

"How about if we take turns scooping it out with seed cakes?" suggested Maddia.

Her suggestion worked, and the family enjoyed the food. The flavor was different than anything they had tried before, and the food was softer, particularly the root vegetables. Maddia shared her food with the wolves, something that her mother did not particularly like. She tolerated it, however, knowing how important the wolves were to all of them.

"Fong said that when we have a problem we cannot solve, we should create a tool that we can use. What tools would let us eat this kind of food better?" asked Tulio.

They were silent for a moment and then Belia said, "Bowls. If each of us had a small bowl, we could pour the food from the cooking bowl. We could probably slurp the food from the bowl."

"With a knife, we could pick up some of the pieces of meat and vegetable," said Lakus. He stabbed at a piece of meat with his knife and put it in his mouth. "We do something like this already with small pieces of meat. The meat is speared with a stick and held over the fire. When it is cooked and has cooled, we eat it."

"And you usually eat it when it is too hot and

yell when it gets in your mouth," said Maddia. "With a bowl of cooked food, you might be more patient."

The news of how Belia and Leeza had cooked the food in a bowl spread around the clan. Others tried it and delighted in the new kind of food. They still cooked in the old ways over a fire, but many meals were cooked in bowls. The people of the Wolf Clan learned that certain leaves, when cooked with other foods, gave the food different tastes. Herbs like bay leaf, rosemary, and sage were commonly added to food cooked in bowls over a fire.

The solution to the eating problem came from a surprising person. Lakus, of all people, became frustrated with slurping the juice and spearing the pieces of meat and vegetable. One evening, as he was about to eat a meal that his mother had cooked, he used a small shell to scoop the food out of the bowl. It proved to be so successful that others in the clan followed his example and ate using shells. Tulio improved the idea by fastening a stick to the shell to make it easier to handle. No one was happier than his brother, Lakus, to have such an efficient eating tool.

Chapter 6

In the vision, Lartha saw the sun go dark in the middle of the day. Shadowy figures approach the camp. They appeared to be lions, but as they drew nearer, she could see they were not. They were humans wearing lion skins. The Lion People had returned.

Lartha woke with a start from her dream state. She was alone in her shelter, which was filled with smoke from burning herbs. The priestess sat motionless for a moment, shut her eyes, and recalled her vision. She knew what she must do. Lartha picked up her staff from the ground and used it to rise. She left the shelter and went to Baratho, the leader of the clan.

"Good day, Lartha," said the leader. He was walking through the camp with several other men and boys. They were guarding the women, children, and elders because most of the men were hunting. The few men who served as guards walked around the camp. They covered the perimeter and passed through the dwellings periodically, always alert for enemies or dangerous animals. Two men sat on a ridge not far from camp to serve as lookouts for anyone coming to the camp from a distance.

"I had a vision, Baratho. The Lion People came back" Lartha spoke carefully in a low voice so the others would not hear. She knew what their reaction would be.

"Come with me," said Baratho, and he pointed toward his shelter. He directed the others to maintain their routines and urged them to be watchful.

"Tell me more," he instructed Lartha once they got to his shelter. Baratho invited her inside, and the two of them sat on the animal skins that lay on the ground. His face wore an expression of concern.

"The Lion People came to our clan. They stole the women and children. They could not be stopped. Events were just as the legend said. In my vision, a dragon ate the sun."

The legend to which she referred had been handed down for generations. The Lion People had been a scourge on the more peaceful tribes for many years. Unlike other groups of humans, they did little hunting or gathering on their own. Instead, they were raiders who would come into a settlement, kill the men, steal what they could, and kidnap the women and children. One day, they vanished without a trace, as if they had never existed. Legend had it that they would return, but only when a dragon ate the sun.

She and others had heard the stories of the sun disappearing from the sky. Some said a dragon had swallowed the sun. Others believed that the moon was challenging the sun as ruler of the sky. No matter what the cause, troubling things were said to happen when the sun was gone from the sky during the day.

"Do you think dragons are real?" asked Baratho. Like the other members of the clan, he had heard stories of dragons, but he had never seen one. Nor had he met anyone who had.

"I am not sure," said Lartha. "Have you visited the dragon cliff?"

"Certainly not," said Baratho. "That is the stuff of legends, too. How could a dragon be trapped in solid rock?"

A story that many people had heard told of a dragon that was embedded in a cliff of solid stone. Not many people had actually seen it, but those who had swore the legend was true. The cliff that held the dragon was in a place that was not very accessible, and the healers from the surrounding clans had marked it with their symbols. Only the most foolish human would run the risk of intruding on such a forbidden place.

"Then we shall go to see it," said Lartha. "If we depart tomorrow morning, we can be there before the sun is overhead. We will be back in camp by evening."

The hunting party had come back that night, so there was no pressing reason for Baratho to remain in camp the next day. He simply said that Lartha had asked him to go on a mission, and they would be back by sunset. No one inquired about the purpose of their trip, especially when Baratho asked Ganni and his brother Piero to join them.

"There is no specific threat," Baratho said to the young men. "I just want to be sure that Lartha is safe, and that she can get help if she needs it."

The journey to the cliff was long but not otherwise difficult. Baratho was surprised at the stamina of the priestess, who despite her years and use of a staff, had no difficulty keeping pace with him and the boys. As she had said, they arrived at the location late in the morning. It was immediately evident to him that they had reached their destination. Objects left by the shamans of many clans were hanging from trees, supported by sticks, or placed on the ground. The vegetation was thick, and no visible trail led into the heart of the forest. Rocky outcroppings stood sentinel behind the trees, some of them topped by conical shapes. Atop a few of them were stones seemingly balanced by unknown forces. There was good reason that people were reluctant to explore the area behind the forest.

"Stay with me," said Lartha. "Be quiet, and do not stray from the narrow path."

Baratho exchanged glances with Ganni and

Piero, who looked wide-eyed at the scene. Had they come to this place on their own, they would never have set foot in the forest. They knew better than to question the magic of the shamans, and this place had been marked by many of them.

Lartha passed between two trees, with Baratho and the boys right behind her. They had no intention of wandering off. The place was unnerving in every way. The shapes of the ridges and the darkness of the forest were bad enough, but when they were combined with the objects left by the healers, the setting became terrifying.

"Where are you taking us, Lartha?" asked Baratho. "This is like no place on our world." Although he was a valiant hunter, his voice trembled as he spoke. He was not embarrassed that the boys heard his fear.

What prompted Baratho's panic was the ground beside the path. In some places, it was muddy, hot, and bubbling. A horrible stench drifted from beneath the surface, which made it difficult to breathe. Neither Baratho nor anyone else at the time knew that these conditions were the result of heat from Earth's interior. To them, a dragon seemed to be a much more sensible explanation of what they saw.

"We are almost there," answered Lartha.

The trail brought them to a sheer cliff and seemed to end. Hidden from their view was a narrow slot canyon barely wide enough for a person to enter sideways. Lartha slipped through the opening, and Baratho followed reluctantly. Ganni and Piero looked at one another anxiously, but they soon gathered the courage to enter the canyon.

The walls were steep, and the conical formations of stone towered above them. Baratho was becoming more uncomfortable. He was relieved to see that the canyon got bigger ahead of them. His relief was short-lived. When he stepped into the open space, he saw something that took his breath away. Embedded in the cliff wall was a dragon, or at least the skeleton of one. The bones of the giant animal were clearly visible. Baratho could not fully grasp what he was seeing.

When Ganni and Piero saw the bones in the cliff, they dropped to the ground. They knelt with their eyes to the ground, afraid to stare for any length of time at the dragon. Despite Lartha's assurance them that nothing would happen, they were hesitant to rise.

"It is not like anything I have ever seen," Baratho whispered. "The legends are true."

"I see no wings on this dragon," said Lartha, "and I do not think it will regain its life. There may be others, and given the size of this one, it is possible that a dragon could swallow the sun."

Stunned by the creature in the cliff, Baratho added, "We must hope that we never happen upon such a beast. May we go now?" He was eager to leave this place.

Like other humans of the time, they did not

know what they were looking at. The buried animal was not a dragon, but the bones of a dinosaur. It would not be for thousands of years that people would discover that giant animals roamed Earth long ago. The legends of dragons, giants, and other mythical beings came in part from humans finding fossil bones.

The four of them retraced their steps. As they were leaving Ganni said to Lartha, "There are no birds or animals nearby. Was this similar to your experience before?"

"Very few, if any, living things are around," she replied. "I do not know if that is because of the stench from the ground or fear of the dragon. The silence here is overwhelming."

The healer looked at the boys and insisted, "You must speak of this to no one. I have great trust in both of you. Do not return to this place without me. If asked, tell the others that we were looking for places to grow the seeds that Piero has collected."

As they made their way back to the encampment, they hardly spoke. Lartha was still concerned with her dream, and Baratho could not get the image of the dragon out of his mind. The two boys, who were normally talkative, said nothing and withdrew into their own thoughts. Their absentmindedness almost brought them to disaster.

Once out of the forest near the dragon cliff, they had to cross a grassy plain. On a typical day, all of them would have been attentive for any signs of danger. Today they were not. Distracted by their thoughts, they did not see the wooly rhinoceros coming toward them.

Somehow, they had managed to position themselves between a male rhino and his mate, who stood with a baby not far away. This awesome beast was more than ten feet long and six feet high at the shoulder. Covered with thick fur from which its name came, the wooly rhino was able to survive the extremely cold climate at this time in Earth's history. It had two horns, with the larger being more than three feet long. Despite its stocky build, the animal was quick on its feet. Usually living in small groups or alone, the wooly rhino was a dangerous prey. Humans hunted it only when they were desperate. Because it was a plant eater, the rhino would attack humans only when provoked, as it was in this situation.

The rhino strode to a position between the humans and its family. Raising its head up and down, it snorted fiercely. The rhino was preparing to charge toward the humans, who would have been no match for it.

"If we run, we can make it to the woods before it is on us," suggested Baratho. "Once in the forest, we will have an advantage. We can probably climb a tree and avoid the rhino."

"I have not run anywhere in years, and I doubt I could outrun a rhino," said Lartha. "And if by chance I made it to the woods, I do not think I could climb a tree. You three may try it if you wish."

Realizing how foolish he sounded, Baratho said, "I am sorry Lartha. I did not think..."

"There is no reason to apologize," said the healer. "Your suggestion was well-intended and would work for a younger person."

Lartha looked at the rhino and thought back over her years. She had seen animals engage in such behavior before. When they were plant eaters, as was the rhino, they were more intent on driving off the perceived threat than engaging in a battle.

"Let us simply walk to the forest," advised Lartha. "If the rhino charges, you can run. It cannot deal with all of us, so most of us will survive."

Looking at Lartha, Baratho and the boys saw a strange expression, something that resembled a smile. Her manner was one of resignation, of willingness to submit to whatever fate might bring her at this moment. As a warrior and hunter, Baratho was not accustomed to such acceptance, and was more inclined to take a strong action. Ganni and Piero, both of whom had shown much bravery in the past, were equally amazed. They knew that the priestess was much more powerful than her frail appearance indicated.

They turned and walked toward the fringe of the forest. Baratho looked over his shoulder and saw that the rhino was still posturing, but it had not moved any closer. The solution that Lartha had proposed seemed to be working. By the time they were at the tree line, all three rhinos had wandered off and were now grazing.

They trekked back to camp through the forest. Once they arrived home, Baratho and Lartha spoke of the encounter with the rhino, but they did not mention the dragon in the cliff. The two boys said nothing. All of them recognized that confirming the legend to others would do more harm than good.

Chapter 7

At different times during the year, the clan visited the story cave. On its walls were drawings that told about the world in which the clan lived and events that were important to them. Checo, the blind storyteller, would recall a story. Some of the clan members would draw while he spoke.

A group of about ten people made the journey on this day. Tulio and the wolf, Albo, walked with Checo. For much of way, the path was wide and smooth because it had been used so often. Tulio would warn Checo of obstacles so he would not trip, and occasionally he would stretch out his arm and put his hand on the boy's shoulder for support.

"You are getting taller, Tulio. It seems like just yesterday when I would put my hand down to touch your shoulder. Now I must extend my arm upward."

"Lakus is just about as tall as I am," said Tulio,

appreciating the compliment that Checo paid him. "And Griffo is now the tallest person in the clan."

Checo leaned down and patted Albo. Because both Albo and Nasha had spent so much time with humans, they had become accustomed to walking beside them. They seemed to be aware of Checo's need for a guide. When they walked with him, they stayed where he could reach down and touch them. Needless to say, the wolves enjoyed the attention.

When they got to where the forest ended, the group stopped. Maddia, Lakus, and Nasha would go to the cave first. No animals lived there, but they sometimes spent the night in the cave. It was better to check the cave before going in rather than to risk disturbing one of the dangerous animals that might be resting there. It was also possible that some wandering humans would be using the cave.

"Everything seems quiet," said Lakus out loud, "and there are no signs of an animal or other people."

"We should walk back and forth in front of the opening before signaling the others," cautioned Maddia.

A growl from Nasha caused both of them to halt. The hair on the wolf's back stood up, and she was perfectly still. Maddia held up her hand as a warning to the others, who withdrew into the forest and hid themselves. Lakus, Maddia, and Nasha ran back to the forest to join them. No one was sure what or who was in the cave.

"Over here," said a soft voice, "behind the log."

Seeing that it was Lartha, they slipped into a dense clump of brush growing around a log. They knelt down beside the priestess in a position that would let them see the mouth of the cave.

The bear that came out of the cave was enormous. It sniffed the air and looked around. Both Nasha and Albo, although they were apart, snarled protectively. The people who had come to the story cave were armed with spears and other weapons. With the wolves to assist them, they could probably have subdued the bear if it turned on them. They hoped it would not, however, so they calmed the wolves and stayed where they were.

To everyone's surprise, Lartha stepped out of hiding and walked from the forest to the clearing. She said nothing and just stared at the bear, which did not approach her. It rose on its hind legs and gazed back at the healer. Those who were close enough heard her words.

"There are few of you left," she said in a friendly tone. "Some day, you will be gone. We shall miss you. I pray your spirit will watch over us always."

Lartha held her hand up with her palm facing the bear. He made a movement that seemed to imitate her as if he was waving goodbye to her. The bear dropped to all fours and walked away from them toward the river. When the bear vanished into the forest, the others gathered around Lartha.

"Were you not afraid?" asked Lakus. "It could have harmed you."

"The cave bear does not eat meat, so it did not see me as prey," answered Lartha. "The bear might have attacked if it sensed danger, but I did not provoke it. Some of us believe that the cave bear has special powers, and long ago, there were many of them. Things have changed in our world, and they seem to be disappearing. The same is true for mammoths and other huge creatures. Maybe it is better for us, I do not know. But it saddens me to think that our great animals will not be here with us."

The group advanced to the cave again, this time more confidently. Because the bear had been inside, it was unlikely that any other animals or humans would be in there. At the entrance to the cave, they lit their torches.

Tulio started a small fire by striking two stones together. He and other clan members carried firestones and pieces of dried plants that would light quickly. The sparks the stones made when struck together lit the kindling, and in a moment, a small fire was going.

Each of the clan members who had a torch lit it from the fire. The torches were made of wood with plant fiber wrapped around one end. This material had been soaked in animal fat, which burned more brightly. The blazing torches were smoky, so the roof of the story cave was coated with soot.

One by one, they went inside. Tulio was among the last to enter. He had done something unusual. He did not have a torch. As an alternative, he had brought a small bowl filled with wax made by bees. The bowl had been a recent invention by Leeza, one of the women of the clan. She had made it out of mud and put it near a fire kept by the toolmaker Fong. When it was removed from the fire and had cooled, the bowl was hard. This container had many uses because it could hold liquids as well as solids.

"Did your idea work?" asked Fong.

"I am not sure," replied Tulio. "It will take a moment."

Tulio's idea came from something that he and Fong had stumbled upon. Wax made by bees quickly melted in a fire and then burst into flames. The boy thought that it burned better than fat and was not so smoky. When torches using animal fat were ignited inside a hut or the cave, the air became smoky and uncomfortable to breathe. He wanted to see if the wax could be used as a kind of torch.

To do this, Tulio asked Leeza for a small bowl made of clay baked in a fire. He put wax in the bowl and set it on fire. It did not burn well. When a small piece of burning wood fell into the wax, however, something interesting happened. The flaming wood continued to burn and melt the wax, which also burned. Moreover, the flame was concentrated around the burning wood and did not flicker over the surface of the wax.

Today, instead of a torch, Tulio wanted to use a bowl of wax in the story cave. He put some burning embers in the middle of the bowl of wax. As he expected, they continued burning and ignited the wax.

"You have done it," said Fong enthusiastically. "You have made a new kind of torch. And look, there is almost no smoke!"

The two of them walked into the cave. Tulio moved carefully so he would not extinguish the flame. Those already inside the cave looked at the bowl he brought. It was much smaller than their torches, and its flame was not as bright. They noticed that it burned more cleanly, and they realized that his flame was better than theirs. For future visits, most of them would bring beeswax in bowls and not the tallow torches they had always used. They would use this source of fire for lighting their huts, too.

The story that Checo told was one that all of them knew. It was about Nasha and the aurochs, the wild cattle that the clan had trapped in a canyon. As Checo told the story, two of the young people, Katia and Piero, drew on the walls. The story had personal meaning for Piero because he had been there when Nasha drove the aurochs into the valley.

"Are the colors ready?" asked Katia.

"Just about," answered Maddia. She was mixing a finely ground red rock with beeswax in a large shell. This technique was one that the clan had used for many years. The mixture of beeswax and pigments was also used to paint their faces and bodies.

"Here is the charcoal," said Evalen to Piero. "It is wrapped in leaves so it will not be so messy when you apply it."

Evalen had brought pieces of burnt wood that she had pulled from the communal fire in the village the night before. Charcoal was one of the oldest things that humans had used for cave drawings and produced black or gray lines and shades. Other colors were made with ground stones or plants crushed with water or wax.

"Can you bring a torch over here?" asked Piero. "This spot feels smooth. I want to see what colors the rocks are."

Tulio held a torch near the wall. This section of the cave wall was light gray, which was ideal for what Piero had in mind. He looked at the pieces of charcoal that Evalen held and chose one that was the width of his thumb. Tulio marked some dots on the wall with the charcoal to give himself an idea of the area he would cover. By adding strokes to connect the smudges, he had drawn a rough outline of an aurochs, including its great horns. He then drew more lines to create an image that anyone would recognize.

"Do you need the red color yet?" asked Maddia.

Return of the Lion People

"Let me see it," he answered. He looked at the powder in Maddia's shell and added, "That shade is perfect. Remember what the biggest aurochs looked like? It had a reddish coat with a black stripe down its back."

Before applying the pigment, Piero stepped back and looked at the outline he had drawn. He wanted to be sure that the proportions of the drawing were true to life. Pleased with what he had done, he reached into his tunic and pulled out a fist-sized ball that was white, soft, and fuzzy. It was made of a cottony fiber he had picked from plants that grew near the settlement.

Piero dipped the cotton into the mixture very carefully. He touched the cotton to the wall a few times to get the shade he wanted. Then he repeated the process several more times. He was patient as he applied the color, making it darker near the top of the animal's back and lighter below. This dark to light pattern was an accurate representation of how many of the aurochs looked.

"Will you draw Maddia and Nasha?" asked Noelo, the younger brother of Evalen. "Checo said they were part of the aurochs story."

"I am drawing Nasha," said Katia. "But we do not draw our people." Knowing that her answer would not satisfy Noelo, she said, "Lartha will explain why we do not draw people."

The boy walked over to Lartha, who was standing where she could see the artists at work.

She had heard the question and was prepared to answer.

"Part of a person, the spirit, cannot be seen," said Lartha. "This spirit is deep inside you. We do not understand it very well. When our life here ends, this spirit may go on. We do not know where it goes, or if it comes back to this world. If we draw a person, we may steal the spirit and put it on the wall."

Noelo said nothing. He just stared attentively at Lartha. Then he asked in a voice loud enough for others to hear, "What is your opinion about that?"

No one else said a word. Katia and Piero stopped drawing. Everyone was listening for Lartha's answer. They were also stunned that Noelo would ask such a question.

Lartha smiled, knowing that the boy's query was well intended. "I am not sure," she replied. "If the spirit is so special that it can survive death, then it may be strong enough to resist being stolen by a drawing. Even so, our tradition is that we may draw other things, but not people. The tradition seems harmless, so perhaps we should keep it alive."

Lartha's answer seemed to satisfy Noelo and the others. They returned to their tasks, and when they had finished the drawings, walked back to the village. On the way, something unusual happened. The ground shook for a brief period, causing all of them a moment of panic.

When the tremor ceased, the young people were concerned about the shaking ground. They had never experienced anything like it. Checo, who had felt the ground shake before, calmed them.

"It is nothing," he said. "The ground shudders from time to time. Sometimes years pass between these events. I have heard legends about giant beasts living under the ground. When they stir, their movements cause the ground to quake." He smiled and added, "This day when the ground trembled under your feet is memorable. It may never happen again in your lifetime."

Checo's words had a soothing effect. The young people could not wait to get back to camp to ask others if they had felt the shaking ground. Checo was wrong, however, about a tremor like this never happening again.

Chapter 8

Many days had passed since the mammoth hunt. Vica, Tali, and Dani were now part of the clan. They still lived with Lura and her father, who doted on the girls. He had never been happier since losing his wife.

One morning, rather than joining the hunters or gatherers, Vica and Lura asked Fong to come to their hut. They showed him something that Vica had been working on. He was baffled as he looked at it. The object consisted of a bent piece of wood that Vica had smoothed. The bend in the wood was maintained by a string made of fibers from the hemp plant.

"It is called a bow," said Lura. "Vica learned about it when she was held prisoner. She says it is a very effective weapon." Lura picked up a straight stick with a sharpened point and a notch in the other end. "This is an arrow, and it is sent through the air by the bow."

Vica took the bow and arrow. She held the bow with her left hand. With her right hand, she put the notched end of the arrow against the string. The arrow rested on her hand. She pulled the arrow back to demonstrate how it worked.

"What an unusual weapon," said Fong, who held out his hands.

Vica gave the bow and arrow to him. Vica helped him hold them properly. She was careful that he did not point the arrow at her or Lura. The toolmaker pulled the arrow back and felt the tension of the bow.

"Please show me how it works." Fong could not wait to learn more about the weapon. As a toolmaker, he was curious about inventions of any kind.

They went outside to where the camp was bounded by a cliff. Vica aimed the arrow and shot it into a place on the cliff that was mostly dirt. When she released the arrow, Fong stepped back and drew his breath quickly. The speed of the arrow was astounding. It startled him because it flew faster than a bird.

Vica retrieved the arrow and showed Fong how to use the bow. He aimed the arrow carefully and let it fly toward the cliff. Once again, he was startled at its performance. His mind raced with the possibilities of the weapon for hunting and defense.

Fong examined the arrow and noted how deeply it had stuck into the ground. Turning to

Vica, Fong said, "You must show me how to make this weapon." He pointed to the tip. "We can put a stone point on it. Come to my shelter, and we will try it."

When they arrived at the shelter, Tulio was there. The boy often worked with Fong and was an accomplished toolmaker himself. Today he was using a technique that he had learned from a friendly clan that had spent some time with them. Tulio had put a stone in the hearth that Fong had built. He waited until it was thoroughly heated and slid it out using a long-handled tool. The heating caused a change in the stone, making it flake more easily than a cold stone. Learning this method allowed him to make tools faster and more precisely.

Seeing Fong and the women approach, Tulio stopped his work on the tool. "Did the three of you come to see how the stones are doing in the fire?"

The women looked puzzled, so Fong clarified what Tulio was talking about. "For some time now, we have been testing stones in a fire. It all began with trying to melt golden stones. We found that some stones changed a little when they were heated in the fire. One kind of stone actually burst into flames."

"Is it the black rock from beyond the cliff?" asked Lura. "I once saw you carrying some back to your shelter."

"Yes," answered Tulio. "The black rock is from

Return of the Lion People

the cliff. For some reason, it is found only in a single layer in the cliff. When we put it in the fire, we were surprised. We never expected a rock to burn."

"Not only that," said Fong, "it seems to burn hotter and longer than wood. Now we burn the black rock in the stone hearth along with wood when we make tools."

Fong showed Vica and Lura pieces of black rock. They looked something like obsidian, a stone from which many tools were made. The black rock was softer and could be broken easily. He pointed to the opening in the hearth so they could see what it looked like when it burned.

"But that is not why we are here. Tulio, wait until you see what Vica has made," said Fong excitedly.

Looking at what Vica held, Tulio was as baffled as Fong was when he first saw it. Vica demonstrated by shooting the arrow at the base of a tree where it could stick in the ground. When she gave him the bow, Tulio touched it as if it were magic. He pulled back on the string while Lura got the arrow.

"The arrow has a point that has been sharpened," said Fong. "What if we put a tip on the arrow as we did with the spear?"

Taking a stone knife, Fong cut a straight branch from a nearby tree. He skinned the bark from the branch and smoothed it. With the same knife, he made a small slit in one end of the branch. Looking on the ground, he found a chip from the stone that Tulio had been working. It was about the size of his thumb, and by striking it with another stone, he refined it into an oval shape with a point at one end.

Fong slipped the stone head into the slit in the arrow. He took a hemp fiber from a basket and began wrapping it around the arrow and the stone. He had a collection of hemp fibers, leather strips, and even mammoth hair because he used them to fasten the heads to spears, axes, and other tools. Looking at the trees, he found one that was oozing sap. With his fingers, he dabbed the sap on the hemp that held the arrowhead in place. If he had time, he would have let it dry naturally over the span of two or three days. Even wet, the sap would act as a kind of glue.

"With the stone head on the arrow, I think it will pierce the hide of an animal more readily." He beamed at Vica as he told her his idea. He added, "Vica, you are brilliant," and gave her a boyish hug.

While Fong was adding the stone head to his arrow, Tulio was playing with the bow. He shot the arrow, brought it back, and shot it a second time. Suddenly his expression changed. He recognized that this weapon would alter the future of the Wolf Clan forever, just as Nasha had.

"How did you think of this?" he said to Vica.

The woman responded with gestures that Lura put into words. She had already heard part of the story from Tali and Dani. "I did not think of it.

While I was a captive, one of my friends made a small one. It was a toy for the girls. We kept it hidden from the guards. The man came from a distant land. He said his people had used the bow and arrow for as long as anyone could remember."

"How far can an arrow go?" wondered Tulio out loud.

"Very far, I think" Vica explained with her hands. She pointed at a tree well beyond the boundary of the camp to demonstrate the distance. "My friend said that warriors could shoot an arrow that far. We never tried."

"Can you help me make one?" asked Tulio.

Vica smiled and shook her head to show that she was willing to assist him. Tulio make a bow. She pointed to a cutting stone and signaled that he should take it. The two of them walked to the edge of the forest behind Fong's shelter. Tulio found a dried stick on the ground about the length of the bow. Vica pointed instead to a sapling. Tulio understood at once that a dried stick would not work, and that a growing tree was needed because it could be bent into the proper shape. He cut the young tree down and carried it back to Fong's workspace.

With the others looking on, Vica showed them how to shape the sapling into a bow. It would be thicker in the middle and tapered toward the ends. Tulio nodded to show that he understood. It would take a long while for him to make the bow, so he would continue at another time.

Pointing to the bowstring, Fong asked, "Does this work well? Have you tried other kinds of twine?"

Vica shrugged her shoulders suggesting that she did not know. "No, hemp was the only long fiber we had."

Fong went into his hut and came out with two strands. One was made from the hair of the wolves, Nasha and Albo. It was finer than the hemp, and he was not sure it would stand up very long to the constant pressure exerted by the bow. The other strand was very different. It was a length of intestine from a wild boar. The piece of gut had been scraped, dried, and twisted. It was very strong and was not affected by moisture. Vica felt it and indicated that she thought it would work well, too.

"We must go," interrupted Lura. She was looking at the shadows on the ground, which was how many people knew the time of day. "We should be guarding the gatherers." She motioned to Vica, and the two of them started to leave.

"Wait, the bow and arrow," said Fong.

"Keep them," gestured Vica. "Use them as a model to make another bow and some arrows."

For the better part of the rest of the day, Tulio shaped the bow. While he worked on the bow, Fong made arrows. Both were patient and paid close attention to details like the taper of the bow from the grip to the tips, the places where the bowstring was attached, the notch in the arrow, and fastening the head to the arrow. Fong made some of the arrows longer or shorter to see if the length altered their distance and accuracy. He also tried wood from different trees and shrubs. By the time the hunting party returned, they had finished the bow and dozens of arrows.

"What is that?" asked Griffo looking at the bow. It was his habit to visit Fong and Tulio after a hunt that they had missed.

"It is called a bow, and here are the arrows," said Fong. "Vica told us how to make them. The bow shoots the arrows. Let me show you."

Fong took the bow and notched an arrow. He chose an arrow with a stone head he had added and aimed it at a tree close by. Griffo watched carefully, but jumped back when Fong released the arrow. He was completely unprepared for what happened and was stunned when the arrow stuck in the tree.

"I cannot believe what I just saw. May I touch it?"

Handing the bow to Griffo, Fong said jokingly, "Do not break it. The force of the bow throws the arrow, not your strength."

Griffo held the bow as Fong had and pulled the string gently and then more forcibly. He looked at Fong, who immediately understood what he wanted. Fong handed him an arrow. The boy set the arrow on the string as Fong had done and let it fly at the tree. He felt a thrill as the arrow left the bow. From that moment on, Griffo dedicated himself to mastering the bow and arrow. He would become a legend among his own people and the clans who lived in the region.

The look on Griffo's face was unmistakable to his friend. "There is no need to ask," said Tulio, anticipating Griffo's question. "Yes, we can help you make a bow and arrows. In fact, we can try something. You are taller and stronger. We shall make your bow a little longer to see if it works any differently."

The three of them wandered among the saplings that grew nearby. Fong chose one that was somewhat taller than Griffo and cut it down. By the end of the next day, Griffo would have a powerful bow and more than ten arrows. In the not so distant future, this new weapon would save many lives.

Chapter 9

Late one afternoon, Tulio dropped by Lartha's hut with Albo at his side. "May we go with you to the place of the stones today?" he asked. Tulio, like the others, was aware that Lartha went to the ridge near camp to identify the longest day, which happened in mid-summer.

"Certainly, Tulio, your company is always welcome, as is yours, Albo." Lartha paused for a moment and added, "You appear to have something to say."

Picking up her staff and some other items, Lartha led Tulio and Albo from the hut. As the two of them made their way up the trail to the high ground, Tulio told her what he was thinking.

"On the shortest day, we raised sunstones. What do you think about raising sunstones for the longest day? Would not the sun be honored?" Tulio looked at Lartha hopefully.

"You are very ambitious," responded Lartha.

"Are you considering three sun stones as we did before?"

"Yes, well..." the boy stammered. "I was thinking of four. Three would be arranged as we did the sunstones for the shortest day. The fourth would go across the top of the two stones facing the sun."

"That is quite a plan," said Lartha. "A longer stone will be needed to cross two standing stones. It will take significant effort to lift such a stone."

"I have an idea," said Tulio.

Tulio set forth his plan to the priestess as they wandered along the path. They climbed to the flat area at the top of the ridge and passed by the three existing sun stones. Not far away, Lartha had fixed a stick in the ground and marked it with her symbol. On the longest day, the shadow of the stick would touch a stone she had put in place the previous year. Each day, she moved a marker stick to track the sun's movements.

"The plan you have described is extraordinary. We should get started as soon as we can. I am sure Baratho would agree."

The two of them and the wolf walked to Lartha's sun stick. She moved the marker stick slightly and saw they had many days to erect the second monument. They made their way back to the settlement and dropped by Tulio's hut to discuss the plan with Baratho, the leader of the clan. Tulio described his plan, and as Lartha expected, Baratho agreed to it. His pride in the boy was unmistakable.

The next morning, Baratho and Lartha explained to the rest of the clan what Tulio had in mind. Recalling the success they had raising the sun stones at the winter solstice, they welcomed the challenge. The clan divided itself into groups to do the hunting, gathering, and raising of the stones. Smaller groups than usual would look for food, but this was not a problem. At this time of the year, there were plenty of animals and producing plants.

It had been two winters since the men of the clan had raised the last group of sun stones, but they had not forgotten their techniques. This time, they had not only their experience, but also the assistance of some of the women and older girls. They thought the task would go quickly, but they did not fully understand what Tulio and Lartha were considering.

A group of young people turned to leave the encampment, but Fong called out to stop them. "Not so fast, my young friends. We need some tools to make the work easier."

The group went to where Fong lived. Unlike most of the others, he had two huts now, one in which he lived and another where he stored tools and supplies. Piled neatly in one corner were ropes, sticks, and logs, all of which had been used to raise the winter solstice stones. Each of the workers would carry something to the site. This was not an easy task, but their pleasant grumbling and complaining made the chore a little more tolerable. So did being with Nasha and Albo, both of whom were pleased with the pack-like behavior of so many humans.

Not far from the place where the raising would take place was a pile of stones. Lartha chose and marked four of them, which surprised those who had helped with the last raising. She did not mention why there was one more than before, nor did they ask. She used her staff to estimate the length of the stones, which were half again as tall as a grown man and as wide as a man's shoulders.

"The stones you have chosen are smaller than the ones we raised before," commented Griffo. "Is that to make our work less difficult?"

"You are as attentive as ever," said Lartha. "And the answer is yes, the smaller stones will make the task easier, but there is another reason you will learn about that shortly.

The new workers, the boys in particular, wondered how they would move such large stones. "I remember your raising the stones before," said Lakus, "but not much else." The boy added, "I was younger then and did not attend to the details."

Everyone laughed at what Lakus said, including himself. The boy was known for not paying attention, yet he accomplished much and was strong as well as being a dependable hunter.

"You will enjoy this," said Griffo. "Your strength will be a great asset. Come over here and

Return of the Lion People

bring your staff."

With the aid of some of the men, Griffo and Lakus lifted the edge of the stone. Fong slipped a log under the stone, and a group of men and women pushed it. As the stone rolled forward, Baratho directed others to put more logs in front. Once the stone was moved a short distance from the pile, ropes were tied to it. Some of the group pushed from behind, others pulled the ropes, and a third crew slid logs in front of the stone to move it to the raising spot.

While this was going on, another group was digging the hole for the stone. Lartha verified the position and made sure that it was deep enough, about a third of the height of the stone. They kept the dirt and stones they removed from the hole nearby but left a flat piece of ground between the hole and the stone.

The hole was finished a short time before the stone arrived. Fong was waiting for it a few paces from the hole where he had placed a thick log. The stone was maneuvered into position by the log. Lartha stood beside the hole and looked at the place where the sun would set on the summer solstice. She thought for a moment, asked Fong to adjust the log a bit, and after he did, told him to continue.

"You two put your spears under the stone," Fong said to Griffo and Lakus. "Lura and Vica, you untie the ropes." As he spoke to the women, he looked at Vica, having learned that she had a remarkable ability to understand him if she could see his lips. At once, she began untying the rope. The stone was now untied and resting on several logs.

Fong said, "On my cue, you two lift the stone high enough to go onto the log beside the hole. Those in the back should push gently so the stone does not go too far. Keep the stone moving straight until I tell you to stop."

Getting down on all fours, Fong looked at the orientation of the stone and the log. He gave the signal to move the stone, and everything went perfectly. The front of the stone rested on the thick log. He held up his hand and rose to his feet smiling.

"Now for the final push," he said. "Four or five of you should be able to move it easily. I will let you know when the stone is balanced on the log."

Those behind the stone pushed carefully under Fong's directions. He showed Vica and Lura how to attach ropes to the back of the stone. They and two others brought the ropes to the other side of the hole, as Fong directed.

"Get ready to push," he told those who were in the back. "The stone will move forward and will slide into the hole. As it does, you push, and those in front will pull on the rope. When the stone is upright, try to hold it steady and we will position it with staffs and spears."

A tiny push was all it took. The stone slid into the hole, just as Fong described. With little effort, it was pushed and pulled into place. Spears and staffs were placed against the stone and wedged into the ground.

"Well done," he said proudly to his team, who stepped back to admire their work. "Lartha, would you ensure that it is aligned to your liking?"

Lartha bowed her head to Fong and walked around the stone. She used a rock tied to a piece of hemp to determine if the sunstone was straight. When she held the end of the hemp, the hanging rock caused the hemp to hang vertically. The priestess asked the workers to move the stone a small amount. When she was satisfied, they pushed dirt and small rocks around the base of the sun stone to maintain its position. Afterward, Baratho led his work group back for the second stone.

"Where should we dig the next hole?" asked Fong.

While facing the hill with the round top, Lartha put her staff on the ground with one end touching the sun stone. "The second hole should be dug under the end of my staff. The depth of the hole is crucial. Dig farther down than is necessary. We can fill it in with rubble in order to adjust the depth so the top of the second sun stone is the same as the other one."

"It sounds as if you have a surprise for us," said Fong. "The heights of the sun stones was not so important during the last raising."

"There is a surprise," answered Lartha, "but it

is not of my doing. After we erect the second stone, Tulio will tell all of you his concept."

The second stone was brought to the hole that had been dug. Before it was raised, however, Lartha used her staff to measure the height of the first stone above the ground, the length of the second stone, and the depth of the hole. She and Fong discussed the height and depth of the second hole. Using a mark on her staff as a guide, they added some rubble so the second stone would match the height of the first.

Most of those who watched were confused by what they were seeing. Baratho asked them to be patient and turned to Tulio and said, "I think it is time that you shared with everyone what you have in mind and how we will accomplish it."

Chapter 10

Feeling a little foolish, Tulio spoke tentatively. "The idea is to put a third stone on top of the two standing stones."

Suspecting there would be a reaction, Tulio said nothing more. His instincts were correct. Most of those clustered around him gasped or mumbled something about it being impossible. Fong, in contrast, grinned and looked at Lartha, Baratho, and Maddia.

"You knew what he would say, and you believe there is a way to do it."

Laughing, Baratho responded, "Let him complete his thought."

The moment of humor lessened the initial doubts of the group. Tulio explained his plan further. "Once the two standing stones are in place, we will lay the third stone beside them. With wooden poles, we will lift one end of the stone. We will place a piece of wood under it and will do the same with the other side. By repeating this, we can lift the lintel stone to the height of the standing stones. Once it is there, we can slide it on top of them."

The confidence with which he spoke was contagious. The skepticism of the group was replaced with a willingness to meet the challenge. All of them realized that if they succeeded, they would be involved in a legendary accomplishment. They spoke with one another enthusiastically, and those who held staffs or spears pounded them on the ground.

Baratho held his hands up to quiet the group. "There is much we must do, and raising the second stone will be a little more complicated than before. We should get started at once."

The process of raising the second stone was almost the same as the first. Lartha and Fong were more precise in positioning the second stone, knowing that it must match the stone that was already in place. The two stones must be the same height, and Lartha wanted the widest sides to face one another.

"Lift the stone onto the log," said Fong. "Push it forward slowly when it drops into the hole. Instead of raising it upright, let it rest on the poles on an angle."

The stone was pushed into the hole and lifted into an angled position. Wooden poles were used to support it. Several of the men and women held the rope attached to the top of the stone. With a series of pulls and pushes, the stone was raised vertically a little at a time. Lartha directed Fong and Tulio to make small adjustments to the stone. Having seen the raising of the other stones, she concluded that it would be easier to arrange the stone's position as it was being raised rather than after it was upright. Once the stone was fully upright to Lartha's satisfaction, dirt and stones were put in place to hold it.

"There is one more thing we should do," said Fong. "We should pack the fill around the base of the stones to make them more stable. We have never attempted to place a third stone on standing stones, and we do not know what will happen."

Using heavy rocks, they pounded the fill around the standing stones. They added more dirt and rubble as the soil was compressed. The rest of the group moved the third stone. Lartha and Tulio wanted it placed precisely. By the time it was in position beside the two standing stones, it was mid-afternoon and becoming too hot to work.

"We will not be able to complete the task in the heat of the afternoon," cautioned Baratho, "so we should stop working for the day and come back tomorrow."

Most of the group went back to the encampment. Tulio asked if he could stay, saying he wanted to prepare the lintel stone, the one that would be placed across the two standing stones. Fong, Griffo, and Maddia volunteered to stay with him, both for protection and to see what he was planning. The two wolves, Nasha and Albo, would be there, also.

"The top stone may slide when it is placed on the standing stones. I think I should make slight pits in the stone. These, plus the weight of the stone, should prevent it from sliding," said Tulio. "The only problem is that I cannot figure out how to make the indentations in the lintel stone."

The four of them discussed solutions until Maddia asked, "Would the rocks we used for packing the ground around the standing stones work? We could pound dents into the top stone."

"That might work, Maddia," said Fong. "Let me look at the pounding stones. Some are harder than others. If we choose pounding stones that are harder than the top stone, I think it will work better."

"I had not thought that stones varied in hardness," said Griffo, "but now that you mention it, surely they do. Some stones crumble easily when struck by others, while our tool stones are very hard."

Fong looked at the rocks that had been used for pounding. He chose several of the larger ones that were a dark gray color. He tested their hardness by striking some of the other stones and found them suitable.

"So, Tulio, where do you think we should make our depressions?" he asked.

Tulio leaned his spear against one of the standing stones with its butt on the top stone. He borrowed his sister's spear and did the same with the other standing stone. With a third spear, he made sure that the distance between the ends of the spears was the same. He then marked the two spots on the top stone by scraping it with a rock.

"You will be taking my position as the clan's toolmaker," said Fong. "I could not have marked them more exactly." From his tone, it was apparent that Fong admired what the boy had done.

Using the hard rocks Fong had selected, he and Tulio struck the top stones on and around the marks. When they became tired, Griffo and Maddia took up the task. The work was tedious, but they made visible depressions in the stone. Fong suggested that they could continue in the morning, and the four of them and the two wolves went back to the camp.

At sunrise the following day, Fong and Tulio left for the site. They pounded the lintel stone until they were satisfied with what they had done. The stone had two cavities that matched the width of the standing stones. They were not very deep, but they would keep the lintel stone in place.

The rest of them cut or gathered logs under Baratho's directions. They were not sure why they needed so many logs, but they were confident the leader of the clan had a good reason. They hauled the logs individually or in pairs to the stone site.

Griffo, who had carried a log alone, dropped it near the top stone and mumbled, "Tulio, I hope you know what you are doing. I cannot imagine how we are going to lift that stone." He smiled at his friend, knowing that Tulio had a plan.

"I thought we could just ask you to lift it," answered Tulio, "perhaps with the added strength of Lakus." He laughed and went on. "But in case you are not up to the task, here is an option. It is probably easier to demonstrate than to talk about."

Fong and Tulio directed Griffo, Lakus, and others to put their spears under the stone and lift one end. When the stone was up, they slid a log under it. The log had been prepared by Fong, who had used a stone tool called an adze to flatten two sides of the log.

They did the same thing with the other end of the stone and lifted it onto a second, flattened log. Once the stone was on the logs, four of them were able to flip it over by using tree limbs as levers. Using the same technique, they slid it along the logs so it was closer to the standing stones.

"We are going to do this several more times," said Fong. "It was Tulio's idea, and I think it will work. By lifting the stone a little and putting a log under it, we can raise it to the top of the standing stones."

"I am not sure," said Lura. "As the stone rises on the logs, it will be increasingly unstable. This happened to us when we started building a hut." As she spoke, she looked at Vica, held her hands up, and moved them from side to side. She was demonstrating how the walls of the shelter they were building had collapsed.

Vica understood what Lura meant because of her gestures. She beckoned at Lakus, and the two of them lifted a log. Lura nodded at the top stone, and the two of them carried it to the sun stone. They put the log beside the sun stone so it rested on the two logs under it. She then picked up two sticks and laid them at an angle against the logs under the ends of the sun stone. As soon as she did, they understood what she was proposing.

"Of course," said Fong. "We need a cross beam on each level and an angled pole at each end so the structure will not collapse. Well done, Vica."

Griffo and Lakus added a log to the other side, and four of them used long poles to lift the rock again. As they did, they realized that by laying the poles on the cross beams, they could elevate the stone even more easily. Because there were no more flattened logs of the right size, they lowered the stone.

"We cannot elevate the stone any more without logs that have been flattened and are the same thickness," said Fong. "If we all work together, we should have enough logs to begin raising the stone higher."

The toolmaker had those with him break into teams. Each team would prepare four logs. He and Tulio went from team to team to explain what they should do. The most important consideration was to be sure that the thickness of the four logs for each level was about the same. The teams worked with cutting stones, adzes, and axes to flatten the logs. It took most of the morning before the work was completed, so they took a break for food when the sun was overhead.

The day was cloudy and cool for this time of year. Baratho asked if they would like to work through the afternoon, and they all agreed. They were excited about raising the lintel stone, something that none of them had ever done or seen before.

After the meal, each group brought its logs. Fong was careful so the logs for each group were kept together because they matched one another in height. Baratho had a plan that he thought would give each group a strong sense of participation in the process of raising the stone. He asked each group, with the help of Tulio, Griffo, Lakus, and Fong, to raise the stone on their logs. He underestimated how pleased this involvement made them feel. After completing their work, each group touched their logs and the sun stone as if they were signing their work.

As each layer was added, the positions of the logs were varied. Vica and Lura put poles at an angle against the rising stack of logs. Between the weight of the stone on the logs and the support poles, the structure remained stable. By sunset, when the tired workers trudged back to the encampment, the lintel stone was just below the level of the top of the standing stones.

When the workers arrived at the site the following morning, Fong and Tulio were already there. The two of them were walking around the standing stones, looking at the lintel stone, and pushing on the logs that supported it to be sure it was secure.

"We are ready to conclude the job," said Baratho. "What would you have us do?" He and those around him looked eagerly at Fong and Tulio.

Tulio answered hesitantly, "Fong and I have discussed options. We might be able to flip it over two times, but there is a gap between the logs and the standing stones. There is also the possibility we could put spears under the stone and roll it, but we are not sure how well we can control its movements." With a sheepish expression, he added, "We are not sure what to do."

Everyone was silent for a moment, and a disappointment seemed to settle over the group. Griffo and Lakus looked at one another and shrugged their shoulders. They walked over to the stone and stood under it. Both boys were tall, so the stone was just about at the height of their eyes. They put their hands on the stone, bent their knees a little, and straightened up. They were able to lift the stone the width of a hand because of their combined strength and the pivot point provided by the log at the other end.

"I think that we can move the stone a few inches at a time," said Griffo. "With a little patience, we can lift it onto the standing stones."

Seeing how easily they had lifted the stone, the others quickly moved over to lend a hand. Fong, however, asked them to wait. "Griffo is probably right, but we must be cautious. The stone is very heavy, and it may tumble over. We have never done anything like this. All of those who are involved must stay near the end of the stone and not trip over the support posts." He pointed at the angled poles that supported the stacked logs.

"The second thing is that we must support the standing stones. Even thought they are large, heavy, and sunk in the ground, we do not know how well they will support the top stone. We cannot brace the standing stones with poles, or someone could trip over them. Some of us will have to lean on the standing stones to hold them up if need be. No matter what happens, if the stone starts to fall, just let it go and get out of the way."

Fong and Tulio directed the lifters. Several of them were at each end of the top stone, and the others gathered around the standing stones. Those under the stone lifted one end and moved it a tiny bit closer to the standing stones. Those at the other end did the same. The work was slow but steady, but because the lifting teams changed members often, no one was overly fatigued by the effort.

The most difficult lift was moving one end of

the top stone from the logs to the standing stone. Many people were handling the top stone while others were supporting the standing stone. It was a little confusing, but the solution became obvious. The edge of the top stone was passed along among the workers until it was in place on the standing stone. The other end was put into position in the same way.

Most of the workers stepped back to look at what they had accomplished. Tulio made adjustments while Fong, Griffo, and Lakus leaned on the standing stones. Tulio placed a wedge of wood under the top stone and tapped it with a rock. This caused the top stone to move slightly, and using this method, the top stone was positioned with its indentations matching the standing stones. The dolmen—two standing stones with a lintel stone on top of them—was complete.

"Should we take the logs down?" Vica asked Fong. She and the others looked optimistically at him and Tulio. They wanted to see the stones without the logs detracting from their appearance.

"I think we have finished with the logs," said Fong, and he looked at Tulio.

"There is nothing more we can do with the stones, so we can take them down," responded Tulio.

The logs were removed carefully, almost respectfully, because they had been such a part of the stone raising. They were carried off and placed with the other implements that had been used to move and erect the stones. There was one more stone that had to be put in place. No one, however, had any idea of the events that would take place before the final stone was in place.

Chapter 11

Where a river flowed into the great sea, several trails came together. People would often meet there to trade or to rest. On this day, two brothers were arguing with some traders from the east.

"What do you mean, you will not trade food for golden stones!" shouted Gortush. "They are the most precious things in the world."

"Apparently not," answered the trader quietly. "You seem to think that our food has more value right now."

"That is because we have been unlucky," responded Jartush. This was not quite true, he knew. Gortush and his brother were not very capable hunters. They had long depended on the skill of others for their food.

"We have knowledge of magic that you may consider to be useful," whispered Gortush. "We know how to charm wolves so they become as tame as children."

The trader looked at the brothers, turned abruptly, and left them. He joined his group, and they set off on the trail that took them toward the sunrise and home. They had heard of the golden stones, but they could think of no reason why they should trade their food for something so worthless.

While the brothers fumed, a stranger approached them. He wore clothes that the brothers did not recognize, and his body was painted in an unusual way. They could not identify his clan from how he looked.

"I will trade some food for your golden stones," said the stranger. "My name is Okar, and I come from near the great sea."

The brothers did not understand all that words Okar said because his language was a little different. They used the words they understood and his expression to make sense of his message. They were surprised at how easy it was to trade with him. They got more food than they expected for a tiny golden stone.

"Tell me more about the wolves," insisted Okar. "I have never heard of such a thing."

"We learned spells that let us change wolves so they behaved like children," bragged Gortush. "Our clan tamed many wolves and no longer had to hunt. The wolves would hunt for us. The priestess of the clan became envious. She stole our spells and turned the clan against us. They tried to kill us, but we got away."

None of this was true, of course. A girl from their clan had raised a young wolf pup that had been left alone. She and the wolf had rescued a second wolf that had no pack. The pair had pups, and the brothers tried to make off with them. The clan had exiled the brothers, and they had been wandering from place to place ever since. They had no real abilities, so no clan was willing to take them in. Gortush and Jartush survived by stealing when they could or trading their golden stones.

"You have been treated unfairly," agreed Okar. "I would like to hear more about this clan and the wolves. You are amazing people to have done what you described."

Okar was not as simple-minded as he sounded. He had met people like these brothers before. They were easily flattered and readily talked about themselves. Much of what they said was not true, but some of it might be. They had golden stones and may know where more were. They may know spells that can enchant wolves. If there was enough truth to what they said, his people could overwhelm the brothers' old clan and take what they had.

"Our father, Ushga, was once chief of this clan," continued Gortush. "We were compelled to move from the sea to the mountains. He abandoned us and the clan. The new leader, Baratho, never liked us. He may have been afraid of my just claim to the position as head of the clan."

As his words expressed agreement and understanding, Okar was thinking just the opposite. He had heard the true story. These brothers stole an animal that had been killed by other hunters. They said it was their kill. The neighboring clans could not tolerate this kind of theft. They demanded that Ushga's clan leave the area. Ushga led them to a valley in the mountains and directed the clan in establishing a camp. When he was satisfied that they were safe, he left in shame at his sons' behavior. He only asked that they be allowed to stay with the clan.

"So you are the true leader of this clan," said Okar to Gortush. Not wanting to offend Jartush, he added, "And you are next in line."

By now, the brothers were beaming. They had found a friend, someone who understood them. They could not hold back from lying about their own accomplishments.

"You will find this unimaginable: we captured a herd of aurochs," whispered Jartush. He looked around so as not to be overheard. "We lured them into a canyon. The clan now has an endless supply of food because of us."

It was true that the clan had a thriving herd of aurochs in the canyon. The brothers, however, had nothing to do with it. The wolf, Nasha, and two of the young humans, Maddia and Piero, had encountered a herd of aurochs. The wolf had driven them into the canyon to protect the children.

Aurochs were huge, cow-like animals that ate grass and other plants. Humans hunted them for their meat and hide, but it was a dangerous task. They had tremendous horns that could gore a human easily. If a herd of aurochs stampeded, they could trample a group of hunters.

"What prevents the animals from escaping, now that you are gone and your powers of magic are not there to stop them?" wondered Okar. His question was sincere.

Gortush responded, "We showed them how to build a wall using small trees, limbs, and branches. It is a sight to behold. The wall stretches across the canyon. There is food in the canyon, and a spring provides water all year."

Neither of the brothers had been part of building the wall that restrained the aurochs. The boys Griffo and Ganni had thought of it. The entire clan except for Gortush and Jartush had built the wall across the canyon. The effort had been successful. The aurochs were content in the canyon. If the natural food supply got low, as it rarely did, the clan brought grass from outside the wall. The aurochs were healthy, and the herd was growing with the birth of new calves.

"The clan that you speak of, where is it located?" asked Okar.

The brothers described the valley where the clan lived. The place was not hard to locate because it was beside a stream that flowed into the river. The clan had erected stones there to honor the sun on the shortest day of the year so it would return the following morning. The sun stones were known to many of the clans.

Okar decided he had heard enough. He listened politely for a short while, thanked the brothers, and left them. Although he knew the brothers were exaggerating their contribution, some of what they said might be true. He would visit this clan to see if they were worth attacking.

When Okar was gone, Valtar stormed up to the brothers. He was a friend of the Wolf Clan, and he had heard what the brothers had told Okar. When he was sure that Okar was far enough away, he growled at the brothers, "You fools, do you know who that was? You have no idea what you have done." He stormed off, fearing what would happen if Okar took their words seriously.

Unfortunately, Okar did take them seriously. Over the next few days, he and a few of his men made their way along the river. They found the sunstones. It did not take long before they were standing on a ridge nearby. Below them was a canyon, and inside was a herd of aurochs, just as the brothers had described. They saw the wall of tree limbs at the end of the canyon and climbed down the ridge toward it. In all their raids, they had never seen anything like the wooden barrier.

Piero came to the canyon, as he did almost every day. Others were with him on this day, but he was the first to arrive. He had become the caretaker of the aurochs. When they needed food, he led the gatherers to the places where he knew there was grass. He had also discovered that if he dropped seeds on the ground, plants grew in those places.

When Piero came to the wall, he tapped on it with a stick. A group of the young aurochs heard the sound and came near him. The older aurochs simply looked at him and continued eating. The younger ones, however, knew that this human brought tasty treats.

"Good morning," said the boy cheerily to the aurochs. "Are we friendly today?"

He held a handful of young plants he had picked through a small opening in the wall. Initially, the aurochs calves just looked at him. Then one of them went to the wall and munched the plants the boy held. When the aurochs became too enthusiastic, he dropped the plants and pulled his hand out. The aurochs was not trying to hurt him, it was just eager to get at the plants.

"Your mother should teach you some manners," laughed the boy. He dropped more plants through the wall, and the other calves nibbled at them. Some were close enough for him to touch, which he did gently.

The boy did not notice the group of men who had descended the ridge. Nor did they want him to. The only way he knew they were near was because the young aurochs suddenly scampered back to the herd. Piero turned, assuming he would see others from his clan. Instead, he saw strangers, and their appearance terrified him.

Okar stared at the boy. He could not let him live. He and his men could do nothing to the aurochs or the clan now, but they would come back with a stronger force. The boy could not be allowed to give a warning. Their assault on the clan would be days away at the earliest.

"Kill him, but do so silently," he ordered one of his men.

As the man drew a stone knife and strode toward the boy, they heard the sounds of humans coming through the forest. They turned, ready to do battle, but saw only young people. This would be no battle, just a bloodbath.

While Okar and his men waited at the base of the ridge, the man ran after Piero, who tried to take off. Standing among the trees at the edge of the forest, Maddia saw the strangers and the warrior chasing her friend. She and her brothers, without regard for their own safety, attempted to rescue the boy. Her brothers headed toward the strangers, while Maddia and the wolves went to Piero and the man threatening him.

The wolves were on the man in an instant. He had no idea they were coming, and his companions were too stunned to warn him. Nasha lunged for his knife arm, caught it in her teeth, and dragged him down. Instinctively, Albo went for his throat, breaking the man's neck in his strong jaws. He lay immobile on the ground, but the wolves did not release him at once. They kept him clamped in their jaws until they were sure he was dead.

Shocked by what had happened, and fearing the wolves would turn on them, Okar and the others fled up the ridge. Maddia, Lakus, and Tulio did not engage them. They held their ground and let the strangers escape. When they were sure the men were gone, they rushed to the wolves.

"Nasha, Albo, come," shouted Maddia. She had to repeat her command in order to get the wolves to leave the dead man. Even as they walked to her, they looked back to be sure he did not move. It was not easy for them to overcome their nature to stay and devour their kill.

"What happened?" asked Lakus. "Who were they?"

Still shaken, Piero answered weakly, "I do not know. When I turned around, they were behind me."

"We must hurry to camp at once," urged Tulio. "Even with the wolves, I would not want to challenge the strangers."

The four of them ran back to the camp. They recounted their story, and some of the older men went to the canyon to be sure the strangers were gone. They inspected the body of the stranger but learned nothing from it. Zibio removed a necklace from the man and brought it back to show the others. They buried the body far from camp and covered it unceremoniously with stones to keep the animals from feeding on it.

Okar and his companions fled, not wishing to risk a confrontation with a group of the clan's fighters. The trip back to their stronghold took several days. Okar had plenty of time to evaluate the words of Jartush and Gortush. Two of the things they said were true. The clan had charmed wolves, and they had contained a herd of aurochs in the canyon. Who knows what else this clan might possess. Okar would plan an assault. He was confident that when his warriors had finished their work, the Wolf Clan would be no more.

Chapter 12

The day after the incident with Piero, Zibio showed the others the necklace that the man had been wearing. When she saw it, Vica turned ashen. It was a single claw from a lion on a leather thong. Her captors had worn the same kind of necklace. Lartha's reaction was even stronger.

"The only clan that is known to wear this kind of necklace is the Lion People," explained Lartha. "I am sorry that I did not ask you more about your captors, Vica. I was concerned about your well-being. It is not a good sign that Piero's attacker was wearing the lion's claw."

Baratho drew Lartha aside. "Is there nothing we can do?" he asked. "Your vision was one sign, and the dragon in the cliff was another. Now we have a third sign."

"All we can do is flee, and where would we go?" responded Lartha sadly. "If we flee, we will be defenseless while we travel, and we would have to leave everything behind. We are not certain that the Lion People will come. Perhaps the experience with the wolves will cause them to stay away. We should prepare for the worst, but otherwise, all we can do is go about our daily routines."

Several days passed without anything strange happening. Scouts sent to other clans came back with little news of the Lion People. There were rumors about their movements, but none of the nearby clans had any other information. Baratho and Lartha began to feel better.

The tenth day after the meeting with Okar and his men started like any other. A sizable hunting group, including the wolves, left in the morning. The women would go out in the afternoon to gather fruit and berries. Baratho and a few of the men stayed in the camp as guards. Mothers with young children and the oldest clan members went about their day as usual.

Although Nasha and Albo were with the hunters on most days, the young wolves were not. They tired easily, and they sometimes wandered from the group. As they matured, they behaved more predictably, and they were at the point where they could spend the day with the hunters. Today, all the wolves were hunting.

Fong was also with the hunters on this day. He wanted to see how well the bow and arrow would work in a real hunt. He was not disappointed. As the group passed from a grassy field to the fringe of the forest, the wolves caught the scent of animals. They began pacing and were eager to pursue the prey.

"Stay with us," whispered Maddia, and she held her hand up to prevent the wolves from moving. She knew that Nasha and Albo would be hold their place, but she was not sure about the other wolves. For now, they stood behind their parents, waiting to see what would happen.

Griffo and Tulio were at the front of the group. Griffo had a bow and arrows, while Tulio carried a spear. No clan hunter had ever used a bow to hunt a large animal, and they were not sure how effective it would be.

Before them, just inside the perimeter of the forest, grazed a herd of deer. They had been alerted to the approach of humans and wolves, but they had not fled yet. Griffo chose a medium-sized stag that was at the outside of the herd. He slowly raised his bow, took aim, and let the arrow fly.

The sound of the bowstring being let go startled the deer, and they took off. By then, however, the arrow had hit its mark. The stag turned to run, stumbled, and fell. The arrow had pierced its lung and heart.

"You did it," exclaimed Tulio, not caring if he caused the escaping deer to run even faster. He looked at his friend with admiration, knowing how long and how often he had practiced.

"It was the weapon made with your assistance," said Griffo, and he held the bow high.

The two of them howled with exhilaration.

The rest of the hunters and the wolves, hearing the sound, ran to the boys. The wolves, especially the younger ones, joined in the howling. When they reached the scene, Tulio was beside the deer, which was about to die. When it did, Tulio touched its shoulder, thanked the deer for the meat it would provide, and wished its spirit well.

Standing up, Tulio said, "The shot was perfect. Griffo must teach us all how to use the bow as well as he did." He looked at Vica and said, "And thank you, Vica, for bringing this weapon to us."

"How did the arrow fly?" asked Fong. He knew that they had some problems with the path of the arrows while Griffo was learning to shoot them.

"The arrow curved a little, as it did when I was practicing. I was able to adjust when I shot the deer." Griffo moved his hand to show the path that he thought the arrow had taken.

Fong, Tulio, and Griffo had tried arrows of different stiffness to test their accuracy. The bow that they carved for Griffo was strong, and it seemed to cause the first arrows they made to bend in flight. Fong had made arrows of varying lengths and different woods until they found a combination that worked predictably.

"And the feathers?" said Fong. "Did they affect the flight of the arrow?"

"I am not sure," answered Griffo. "I was more intent on the target."

Tulio added, "From what I saw, the feathers kept the arrow from wobbling too much. I think we should continue adding them to the arrows."

The arrow that Griffo shot had feathers on the end opposite the head. This was a suggestion made by Leeza, who thought that the tail of a bird seemed to help it fly straight or change direction. Fong had attached the feathers to the arrow with a glue made from pine sap and then wrapped them with strands of mammoth hair. It was painstaking work, but the result was worth the effort. The bow and arrow would prove to be an extraordinary weapon for the Wolf Clan.

Because the day was still early, they decided to hang the deer from a tree, gut it, and carry on with the hunt for more game. The wolves, agitated by the scent of the deer, were eager to run. Maddia gave Nasha the signal that she could follow the deer herd, and the wolves took off after them. Maddia and Lakus trotted after the wolves, not letting them get far away before calling them back. The deer were by now out of comfortable range for the wolves, but tracking them was a good training exercise. It was only then that they and the other hunters noticed that the day had become unusually gloomy. Within a short time, what they saw in the sky would cause them to end the hunt and rush home filled with terror.

Back at the camp, Lartha and Checo were planning a trip to the story cave the next day. Dani and Tali were grinding the pigments that would be used to draw pictures on the walls of the cave. The chips of colored rock were placed in a flattish stone with a cup-like indentation. With another stone, the girls crushed the chips into a fine powder.

They sat in the open area near the great fire. It was now just smoldering, fed with an occasional stick. The clan had found that allowing the fire to burn with a low flame during the day was more efficient than restarting it each night. The smoke generated by the low fire was also used to preserve meat and fish.

"What story will you tell?" asked Dani.

"We will tell several stories," answered Checo. "One will be about you. We will tell of the mammoth hunt and the lion that stalked you."

Tali said, "I remember that day. We were starving, then we were afraid. We thought the lion would get our mother. You saved us. We could not believe that wolves and people were friends. Now it is like a dream."

"Things have a way of working out for the best," said Checo. "Your coming to us was a gift. Vica has been a dear friend, and the two of you are like my children. Our clan is better because you are with us."

The sky had become cloudy, suggesting that it might rain. As they worked, the day became darker, and Lartha looked at the sun. Between the breaks in the cloud, she saw something that sent a chill down her spine. Part of the sun looked as if it had been eaten away. She waited for a moment, hoping that her observation was wrong, and that a cloud was simply blocking the sun. As the clouds came and went, her concern rose. The sun was disappearing from the sky.

"Stay here," she insisted. "I must find Baratho. I shall be back shortly."

Lartha hurried to the perimeter of the camp where Baratho and several men were standing. They, too, were looking at the sky.

"This cannot be," he muttered to Lartha. By then, it was evident that something was happening to the sun. Baratho thought of the vision Lartha had shared with him.

"Take the women, children, and the old ones to the hiding cave," commanded Lartha. "I will bring Checo, Dani, and Tali to my shelter." She added regretfully, "I pray my vision is wrong."

By then, everyone in the village was on the verge of panic. The sun was being swallowed up before their eyes. The partial cloud cover made it impossible to tell what was happening. They did not know if a dragon was eating the sun or the moon was taking the sun's place in the sky. For all they knew, their world was ending.

Baratho and his guards hurried the women with young children and the elders toward the secluded cave. This was a safe spot known only to the clan. The entry to the cave was a narrow crevice in the cliff beside camp. It could be easily disguised by branches.

The women with older children waited for their chance to enter the cave. Once all those who needed assistance were inside, they would go with them. Unfortunately, that chance never came.

Lartha, Checo, and the girls arrived at the shelter. By then, most of the sun was obscured. Lartha described what was happening for Checo, who remained relatively calm thus far. He could not see the sun vanishing, so he was not affected as much as the others. His composure made Dani and Tali feel somewhat more relaxed than they would otherwise have been.

Alek, the father of Lura, had been instructed by Baratho to keep watch from a rocky outcropping just outside of camp. From there, he could see in every direction. As he looked around, he saw two groups marching toward the camp. Because of the poor light, he initially thought they were the hunters. Then, as the sun started to emerge, he saw what the men in front were wearing. His heart raced and his knees felt weak. Some of them were clothed in the skin of a lion, and he knew that the Lion People had returned.

Without leaving his post, Alek shouted a warning. As soon as Baratho heard his words, he realized that Lartha's vision was coming true. A dragon had not swallowed the sun, but the Lion People were almost upon them. There would be no time for all of them to hide in the cave. He told the women and older children to run off in the other direction. He and his guards would conceal the mouth of the cave. If they had time, they would flee, too. Baratho knew they would be no match for the Lion People.

One of the women, Dorota, stopped Baratho. "Alek said it is the Lion People who are coming. Is he correct?"

Baratho looked at her, but did not answer. His silence was enough for Dorota. She did not go with the other women. Instead, she headed toward Alek.

"Where are you going, Dorota?" asked Baratho. "You should be with the women. Ducatha needs your help with the children."

"What Ducatha needs is more time to escape," said Dorota. She looked at Baratho with a determined expression. "I know the stories of the Lion People. I choose to die rather than let them get my daughter and her children. Goodbye, my friend."

Dorota climbed the ridge where Alek was standing. She picked up a large rock, as did Alek. When the Lion People were on the trail below them, they hurled the rocks. The invading warriors retreated, not knowing how many people opposed them. Seeing just two people, they came after them.

"Run, save yourself," shouted Alek. "You can go around the ridge to the river. You have a daughter and grandchildren."

"So do you," responded Dorota, and she threw another boulder at the attackers. Those words were her last. Both she and Alek were the first victims of the Lion People.

With the mouth of the cave concealed, Baratho had a decision to make. They could beat a hasty retreat, or they could face the Lion People. Thinking that the women and children needed more time to get away, he decided to take them on. He and his guards ran to engage them as far from camp as they could.

One guard was left by the cave. Kavin, whose family was inside, had a special task. If the Lion People came into the camp, which was likely, he was to distract them from the cave. He waited a short distance from the opening, hoping for a miracle.

The defenders encountered the enemy in a small clearing beyond the ridge on which the corpses of Alek and Dorota lay. The battle was an unfair match. As they usually did, the Lion People struck with an overwhelming force. Baratho and his guards fought valiantly, but they all fell before the might of the Lion People, who lost just a few of their men.

Seeing what had happened, Kavin knew what he had to do. He made as much commotion as he could as he ran from the secret cave toward a ridge by the stream. The fighters saw him and set off after him, just as he hoped. He distracted them from the cave, but paid for his bravery with his life. His sacrifice was worthwhile, for when the Lion People left his body, they went back to the

Return of the Lion People

camp through another route, thus missing the entrance to the cave.

Unfortunately, the Lion People had arrived at the camp from two directions. The women and children who were trying to get away from the camp were intercepted by the second group of enemy fighters. None of them were killed or injured, but being captured by the Lion People was a worse fate.

"The women and children should stay here," said Okar, the leader of the Lion People. "If any of them try to run, kill them."

With two escorts, Okar walked through the camp to the other group of warriors. Seeing that they had done away with the armed clan members, he ordered his men to ransack the camp and take anything of value.

Speaking to Dikach, the second in command, Okar said, "Look for some strips of leather or vine. There must be some in the camp. Have our men tie up the women and children. Then come back to me."

Dikach nodded and went from hut to hut gathering lengths of leather, vine, and a different kind of strand made from animal fur. He took them to the guards who were watching the women and children. The guards bound their hands together and then tied them to one another.

When Dikach returned, Okar's warriors were already pillaging the huts. They took anything useful that they found, including tools, weapons, animal skins, and food. The warriors traveled light, and they would make the captives carry the plunder back to their stronghold. Some of the men took burning sticks from the great fire and ignited the huts.

While his warriors looted the camp, Okar wandered around. He thought that the men and some of the women from the clan were hunting. But where were the elderly people and the mothers with young children? The children that they had captured were relatively old. No babies were among them. He was convinced that others were somewhere in the vicinity. Some of the clan's most valuable possessions could be in the same place.

The enemy warriors who had come from the opposite side of camp claimed that there was no place for survivors to hide. They did not realize that Kavin's death had a purpose, and that they had been deceived. Okar still was not satisfied.

"Dikach, when we have finished with the village, I want to persuade one of the women to tell us where the hiding place is. There are no elders or young children among the captives. They must be somewhere around the camp, and with them might be the valuables of the clan."

The look that Dikach gave his leader suggested that he would enjoy making one of the women talk. He bowed to his chief and wandered back to where the captives were being held.

Chapter 13

The women captives had their hands bound with strips of leather or pieces of vine, as did some of the bigger boys and girls. The other children were tied to their mothers. They were guarded by warriors who treated them mercilessly as they were marched from the camp.

Despite his doubts, Okar had found no signs indicating where the clan members were. Frustrated, he passed through the devastated camp to where the women and children were being held.

"Take them across the stream," said Okar. "Keep them there until I come back. I want to find the sorceress who is supposed to live here. I have heard that she knows about enchanting wolves. Then I will select a child to torture until the mother tells me where the secret place is."

Okar scanned the surroundings, not even sure what he was looking for. The traitor, Gortush, who had once been part of the clan, had been an important source of information about this and other settlements. He said that the healer had magic potions and amulets. Perhaps they would protect him and his men from weapons. He implied that she may even have a cache of gold hidden somewhere. Gortush described her hut, but he did not provide exact directions about its location. It was near the stream and beside a steep cliff against which her shelter was built.

Seeing a possible location, Okar walked to it. As he drew near, he noticed unusual objects hanging from trees and set into the ground, exactly as Gortush had detailed. Okar picked up his pace, confident that he had found the priestess.

Always alert for treachery, Okar paused just outside the hut and looked around. He grasped a stone knife in his hand and burst through the leather flap that covered the opening. The hut was poorly lit, and it took a short time for his eyes to adjust to the darkness. Herbs, bones, and other items that a healer used were hanging from the sides of the shelter. The air was rich with exotic smells. A woman, two girls, and a man stood facing him, none of whom seemed surprised by his entrance. They said nothing, and the girls slid behind the woman, who was undoubtedly Lartha.

"You are just as Gortush and Jartush described, Lartha," hissed Okar as he glared at the woman. He moved slightly to his side and observed the man who was leaning on his staff. The man's eyes did not focus on Okar. "And you must be the storyteller, Checo."

The words that Okar spoke were not completely understandable to Checo and Lartha. His language was similar to theirs, but it was not identical. They knew the meaning of enough of the words and his tone to recognize that they were in danger. Tali and Dani, however, knew what he was saying because they had spent their lives as slaves of the Lion People.

Okar surveyed the inside of the hut but did not move from where he was standing. Gortush was right. The woman's collection of potions, talismans, and such might prove to be powerful. He had never seen such a rich hoard of healer's goods.

"You have done well for me, sorceress," said Okar. "You can die knowing that I will put your potions to good use as we overcome your neighbors. Not that we need assistance. Your clan and the others nearby are so set in your peaceable ways that our slaves could conquer you."

Lartha spoke calmly, but she knew that her words would have little effect on Okar. "I am no sorceress. I am a healer of body and spirit. All that you see around you is meant for the good of our people. What I have gathered will not help your conquests."

"We shall see, witch. And as for you, blind one, you shall die first. I normally would dispatch the woman before you so that your dying memory would be an unpleasant one. With your sightless eyes, her death would mean little to you. I may let the girls live, or I may not." An ugly smirk crept across Okar's face.

Throughout Okar's speech, Checo did nothing other than listen carefully. He attended to every movement the man made. Coming closer to Checo, Okar reached across his body, intending to slash the blind man's throat with a single backhand sweep of his blade.

Without a sound, Checo whirled in a circle, striking Okar in the ribs with his staff. The speed and strength of his assault was remarkable, and the sound of cracking ribs shattered the silence. Okar grunted in pain and surprise, incapable of issuing a scream because Checo's blow had knocked the air out of his lungs. As his right hand, which held the blade, came to his side in a reflexive response, Checo spun in the other direction and brought his staff against the side of Okar's head with a sickening thud. The leader of the Lion People was dead before his body fell limply to the ground.

Lartha took several cautious steps toward Okar's body and nudged it with her foot. "He is dead, Checo. You have lost nothing of your fighting ability, my friend. Why these men of violence underestimate us I will never understand. The girls and I are grateful to you."

Breathing deeply to calm himself, Checo

sighed, "Taking the life of another human is a terrible thing. I knew of no other way to save you and the girls. Please do not think less of me."

Tali and Dani rushed to Checo and hugged him. He wrapped his arms around them, but he never dropped his staff, fearing that another of the warriors would enter the hut.

"We must leave this place before the others search for him," said Checo.

"There is a narrow cave behind the shelter," replied Lartha. "The entrance is concealed by brush. We can go through it to the trail that follows the cliff. With luck, we can escape unseen. Before we go, I have an idea for the body. Come with me girls. We will not be long, Checo."

Each family and individual in the clan kept sticks of various lengths beside their huts. The sticks served many purposes, from holding food over a fire to supporting extensions of the shelters. Lartha chose several long sticks and had the girls bring them to the front of the shelter. While they did, she dragged Okar's body outside.

With Tali and Dani as assistants, Lartha inserted some long sticks into the back of Okar's tunic. She secured the sticks with strips of leather and tied other sticks to his arms. The three of them pushed his body upright on the sticks and arranged them so he appeared to be floating a small distance above the ground. Lartha hoped that if any of the Lion People came looking for him, their superstitious nature would cause such terror when they saw him that they would flee.

Lartha directed the girls to go into her hut and said, "Come, children, we must be on our way." Once inside, she described in detail what they did with Okar's body. Lartha took Checo's arm and led him out of the hut and to the cave. The girls accompanied them, holding on to the end of Checo's staff, which he held behind him. Without even a whisper, the four of them pushed back the brush and slid through the narrow opening.

After a few paces, Lartha stopped, as did the others. She slipped by them and went out of the cave. She swept the ground with a branch to remove their footprints and backed into the cave. She repositioned the shrubs growing near the opening so that no one who was unfamiliar with the cave would notice it.

"Checo, you must lead us now," she said. "I will be behind the girls. The cave is dim, and I do not want to bring a torch. The cave turns gradually to the right, and there are stones and small ledges on the ground."

"It will be no problem for me," responded Checo softly. He began moving forward slowly but steadily. "When I let go of the staff, you girls should hold it in position. I may need both hands in some places."

Although unfamiliar with the cave, Checo was confident. He slid one foot after the other, while at the same time moving his hand and arm in front of him. In some places, he had to release the staff

Return of the Lion People

in order to feel the sides of the cave with both hands. This was especially necessary where it became very narrow with sharp rocks protruding from the walls. When he let go of the staff, Tali and Dani held it as if it was the most important thing they had ever done.

Their journey through the tight cave did not take long. When they got to the other end, Lartha said, "Wait, Checo. Let me see if there is anyone outside."

Proceeding past the girls and Checo, Lartha edged her way to the opening. She listened for a moment and then peered out through the bushes. She saw and heard nothing, so she pushed the bushes back to look around. There were no humans anywhere to be seen. Lartha went back into the cave and led Checo and the girls out.

"Where do you think we should go?" asked Checo.

"For now, nowhere," answered Lartha. "We should say here until dusk. With the cliff at our back and the cover provided by the plants, we can see anyone coming this way, but they cannot see us. I can also climb up the cliff to see if the Lion People are still here. They must be anxious to be on their way, knowing that the hunting party will be returning soon. If need be, I can pass through the cave to my shelter to get food and furs to keep us warm through the night."

At the mention of food, Checo realized that the girls might be hungry. He pulled a seed cake from his tunic, broke it in half, and gave it to the girls. Dani ate hers quickly, but Tali just nibbled at hers. When her younger sister finished, she offered her piece to Dani. The younger girl reached for the seed cake eagerly, but just as she was about to grab it, withdrew her hand. She knew at that moment that Tali had not eaten so that she could have more.

"I have had enough for now," said Dani. "You eat that, sister."

Tali broke her piece in two, handed one to Dani, and ate one herself. Lartha smiled at both girls, as did Checo, because their words and actions showed that the girls were already showing concern for others. This trait had emerged in humans many generations before and had contributed to their survival and advancement.

"Here is what I suggest," said Lartha. "Tali and Checo will stay here and be on the lookout in case any Lion People come through the cave or approach from the camp. Dani can help me ascend the cliff. From the top, I can see the camp and perhaps observe what the Lion People are doing. If we are fortunate, they will be on their way back to wherever they came from."

"Will you be able to climb the cliff?" asked Checo.

"There is a suitable trail," she answered, "and it is neither too steep nor too rocky. With Dani at my side, I should be fine. We will not be long."

Despite being concerned about their situation, the girls were pleased that they had been entrusted with vital roles. Tali moved to Checo's side, and he put a hand on her shoulder. Lartha and Dani walked the short distance to the base of the trail. They looked back once before beginning their ascent. All four of them knew that even though they were safe for now, the situation could turn perilous at any moment.

Chapter 14

While Lartha and Dani scrambled up the path, Checo and Tali sat by the exit of the cave. Tali was able to look through the bushes and trees that grew around the spot. To pass the time, Checo asked her about the Lion People and their language. Tali told him the names of everyday things like foods, tools, clothing, and such. Checo asked her about expressions, descriptive words, and any of the stories that she had heard during her captivity. He was surprised to learn that the girl knew not only the words of the Lion People, but of other clans as well because so many people had been captured.

Lartha and Dani made it to the top of the cliff. The priestess motioned for the girl to lie down on her belly, and she did the same. The two of them crawled silently toward the rim of the cliff, trying to stay behind boulders and small bushes.

"Stay near me," said Lartha. "If I stop, you must

do the same. Remain as flat as you can. We do not want them to see us."

When they got to the edge of the cliff, the scene that greeted Lartha was disturbing. In the village itself, there was no motion at all. No one was around. Many of the huts were destroyed, and some were on fire.

Near the side of the village beside the stream, the Lion People had gathered the women and children together. It was an appalling image that filled her with dismay. As she stared forlornly at her friends being prepared for a punishing march, she almost missed seeing the person walking toward her hut. One of the Lion People had split off from the others, probably looking for Okar.

"Get down," Lartha whispered to Dani, but it was not necessary. The girl was as flat to the ground as she could get. Lartha peered from behind a nearby bush to watch the man, hoping he would not look in her direction. Trees were overhanging the path in most places, and they lessened the visibility.

Dikach walked confidently, believing that no one was left in the camp. He was not sure where he was going, but he took the path that Okar had followed. The winding path was overgrown with plants on both sides, so he could not see more than a few steps ahead.

As he got closer to Lartha's shelter, the path made a final turn before it widened into the clearing around her hut. At the clearing, Dikach he froze in terror. The mighty Okar had not only perished, but his body was suspended magically in the air. A spell of the priestess must have killed him and left him in this horrible pose. A scream rose in his throat, and he ran back toward the captives and his companions.

Before Dikach arrived, the rest of his band heard his howling. They were prepared for an attack, but not for the story he told them. The ghastly sight he described caused a panic among the Lion People. There was no talk of torturing any of the prisoners to obtain information about the secret place. They shoved and prodded their captives to get them to move as quickly as possible away from the camp. In an instant, the Lion People had been transformed from proud warriors to fleeing captors with women and children as their prisoners.

"What did he say?" asked Dani.

Smiling, Lartha replied, "I could not hear him, and even if I could, I would not understand all his words. I suspect that he is blaming me for their leader's dreadful end. I hope that some day they learn the truth, that it was not I who did him in, but a blind storyteller."

The two of them stayed where they were until the Lion People and their captives marched out of view. Even then, they got up cautiously and concealed themselves as well as they could in case a few warriors lagged behind. The pair walked along the trail, descended quickly and quietly, and returned to Checo and Tali. They described what they saw, although Lartha did not provide many details about the camp in order not to upset them. She thought that the four of them should walk to the camp to see if there were survivors.

They did not speak at all as they made their way to the village. They were dismayed when they saw the damage, but puzzled by what they did not see: not a single person, living or dead, was in the camp.

"How can that be?" asked Checo. "You said that the Lion People had taken just the women and children."

"That is true," said Lartha. "Checo, you and Tali wait here. Dani, come with me."

Lartha and Dani rushed to the far side of the camp. The plan was for the women and older children to hide the mothers with very young children and the older people in a cave. An outsider would be unlikely to find it. Lartha looked around and saw no one. She and Dani removed the leafy branches from the mouth of the cave. Not a sound could be heard from the inside, and the interior was pitch black."

"It is Lartha. They have gone. You may come out."

For a terrifying moment, there was no sound, and Lartha thought the worst, that no one had made it to the cave. But then came a shuffling sound, and Shara came to the entrance. Behind her and holding on to her clothing were Conor and Ralin, her children. She turned to the side, as did the children, and her grandmother came into view, walking gingerly and leaning against the wall. Shara held out her arm for the older woman, and the four of them left the cave. Dozens of others walked out, all with the same blank expression. They found it difficult to comprehend what had happened, and they did not yet know the full extent of the disaster.

"Come, let us go back to the settlement," said Lartha. "But be prepared. It is not the place you will remember."

The group moved slowly along the trail, assisting one another as well as they could. Even though Lartha had attempted to prepare them, they were dismayed when they saw the camp. Most of the shelters had been damaged in one way or another, and some had been completely destroyed. Those who were able tried to put out the small fires that were burning. They carried animal skins to the stream, wet them, and smothered the fires. Fortunately, there was little vegetation on the ground to burn, so the fires that had been set by the Lion People were confined to the shelters that had been ignited.

"We must identify the places that are livable so we can spend the night," said Lartha. "But before we do, I have a favor to ask of you. While the events of the day are fresh in your minds, tell Checo all that comes to mind. We must never forget what happened to our people."

As she walked past Checo, Lartha squeezed his arm. He nodded to show that he understood why the priestess had asked the survivors to tell their stories to him. Describing what happened would let them feel that they were doing something to hasten the clan's return to normal after such a tragic day. Her suggestion had the effect she had intended. Shara guided Checo to a log where he could sit and listen to the clan members, and they were quickly gathering around him.

After all the stories were told, Lartha spoke to the group. "We will have to share our huts tonight. I trust that those of you whose homes are undamaged will welcome others."

"Of course we will," said Shara quickly. "I can see that our hut has been damaged only slightly. The children and I would be honored if anyone in need would join us."

Others spoke in agreement, and the clan members helped one another into the huts that were intact. Lartha would share her hut with Checo, Tali, and Dani. She could take in more people if necessary, but it seemed as if everyone had a place.

Before they went to her hut, Lartha thought she should check to see that they all had food. She was about to leave when Checo said, "Wait, I hear something."

At first, Lartha heard nothing, nor did the girls. They stood still, then the three of them heard the sound. It was voices, and they were getting louder.

They could not tell what the voices were saying, but they all had the same fear. They might belong to the Lion People.

The girls went to Checo and moved behind him. Tali and Dani looked cautiously in the direction of the voices. Lartha was at Checo's side. Each of them had a staff, but otherwise they would be powerless against the Lion People. There was nothing they could do to defend themselves or the others.

Nasha and Albo bounded into the encampment, with Griffo and Tulio just steps behind. Shortly after them came the rest of the hunting party. Speechless, they stared at what was left of the camp. Because the hunters had taken a path that had not been used by the Lion People, they had no idea what had taken place.

"We thought the sun was going to vanish," said Tulio, "so we rushed back as soon as we could. Did the sun's disappearance cause this destruction?"

"The Lion People attacked while you were gone," said Lartha. "They captured some of the women and children. The elders, the youngest, and their mothers hid in the secret cave and are fine. They are in the huts." Lartha hesitated for a moment. "I do not know where Baratho and the others are."

"We must go after the hostages!" urged Griffo. "The Lion People cannot get away with the women and children. There is no time to wait. They will be impossible to find after nightfall."

"It is already too late in the day," said Lartha. "We will not catch them."

"Then we must look for Baratho and the guardians at once," declared Zibio. He pointed at some of the hunters and said, "You stay here. The rest of you come with me. We will start at the secret cave."

As the party left, the women, babies, and elders came out of the huts. They had stayed inside until they were sure that the voices they had heard were clan members and not Lion People. Some of the fathers who were going with Zibio were relieved to see their wives and children, but they knew they had no time for each other now.

Maddia and Griffo stayed at the encampment along with Nasha and Albo. The wolves would be a deterrent if any of the Lion People returned. They and the other hunters spread out to the fringes of the camp. They stayed within shouting distance of one another in case there was a problem.

Zibio and his searchers dashed down the path to the secret cave. There was no sign of Baratho's group anywhere, which was to be expected. Baratho would have taken great pains to hide any evidence so those in the cave would not be discovered. The search group stayed on the path to where the cliff ended. They were overwhelmed by what they encountered. On the ground were dozens of bodies, including Baratho, some of the clan's elders, and warriors of the Lion People.

Under ordinary circumstances, they would have gone through a grieving ceremony, but there was no time for that now. The sun was setting, and the predatory animals would soon be prowling.

Falling to one knee, Zibio put his hand on Baratho's shoulder. He bowed his head for a moment and said, "We must take them home and bury them with honor."

"What about the dead Lion People?" asked Tulio. "We cannot just leave them."

Despite the grumblings from some of the others, Zibio agreed with his son. He was willing to bury the Lion People not because they deserved it, but to keep the clan safe. If the corpses stayed on the ground, they would attract bears, lions, and wolves. In addition, the spirits of the Lion People might linger near the camp, and the clan would never be free of them. Zibio's respect for other humans included those who had harmed them.

Knowing the area well, Zibio pointed to a small niche in the cliff. "We can put the Lion People in there and seal the opening with stones. Our actions will encourage their spirits to move on."

Although they were reluctant to perform the task, the hunters dragged the bodies of their enemies to the niche. The space inside was small, so Zibio sat them against the wall shoulder to shoulder. He did so to give their spirits peace so they would move on. The burial chamber was sealed with stones. At some time in the next few days, Lartha would come to the niche and mark it so the bodies would be untouched.

The fallen were carried home with as much reverence as the situation would allow. While the hunters walked, they sang the sorrowful chant of passing. The clan members who were waiting at camp heard them long before they arrived. They knew what had happened.

Chapter 15

They made a fire that night around which many of the clan slept. The elders, mothers, and youngest children tried to sleep in shelters, but their rest was fitful. Through the night, they woke and wandered back and forth between the fire and the shelters. Some adults and young people napped by the fire, taking turns as sentinels. Not far from the fire lay the bodies of those who had given their lives to protect the camp.

When morning came, no one was very talkative, other than Maddia. She took the wolves around to the families with children. She knew how much the children loved the wolves, and playing with them made the day a little easier.

"You are doing a good thing," said Belia to her daughter. "The wolves are bringing joy to the children."

"I remember the day that Baratho decided that I could keep Nasha," said Maddia. "When we walked home, the children were quick to accept Nasha. This is a good time for the wolves to repay the favor."

The burial ground of the Wolf Clan was on a ridge near the river. It was a comfortable distance from the camp, neither too far nor too close. Their dead were conveyed to the spot with reverence and were interred in shallow graves over which stone and dirt were piled. The people of the Wolf Clan showed respect for their departed just as they did for the living.

On this day, the burials did not follow the clan's tradition, which was to inter people in individual graves, the exception being when family members died together. Instead, Lartha decided that the slain should be entombed with one another. She believed that their spirits would take the last journey together and console one another.

A grave large enough for all of them was dug. Baratho was placed in the middle and the others were arranged around him. They were buried with their weapons, food wrapped in leaves, and gifts. Family members placed other things with their loved ones, small objects like a shell necklace, tool, or even a clay figure made by a child or friend. Leeza left with Baratho a small bowl she had made and he had admired. Some of the families painted the faces and bodies of those who perished with the colors they used in the story cave.

The surviving members of the clan stood around the site and sang the chant of goodbye. To them, the spirits of the dead were going on a journey, but no one knew where. As the clan chanted, the wolves howled. Everyone experienced a great loss, but they also felt hopeful. Those who fell the day before were good people, and while their remains were returned to Earth, their spirits would continue in another place. Of that they were sure.

The rest of the day was spent covering the bodies of the slain defenders with dirt and stones. All who were able participated in the burial. The mound they built got higher and higher, much more than was needed to safeguard the bodies from animals. Creating the mound became a mission in its own right, and it rose until it was taller than a man. When it was completed at the end of the day, the clan was exhausted but satisfied that they had sent the spirits of their kin on a glorious journey. The mound they made would not be a place of sadness, but of remembrance.

On the way back to camp, Griffo walked with Lartha. Knowing how friendly she and Baratho were, he said, "You will miss him." Her answer, which she did not give immediately, surprised him.

Lartha thought about Baratho, who was more than just her friend. He had done much for the clan over the years, but the most crucial had been the simplest. He had not only declared that it was in everyone's interest that food be shared, but his influence had caused people to feel that it was a privilege to do so. The members of the clan least able to hunt and gather—the weak, the old, and the infirm—did not have to beg or eat whatever was left after others had consumed their fill. When the clan ate together, all the members had an equal portion, as they did in families. This set the Wolf Clan apart from some other groups, but those tribes that lived nearby had adopted the same practice.

"Baratho will always be with us," she replied, "as will the others. We speak of him now, and I am aware of his presence. Others, I am sure, are talking about their loved ones who fell. When you are hunting tomorrow, you will turn to Baratho as you approach the prey, waiting for his signal. He will not be there, but you will know what to do. At the fire one night, you will choose a fine piece of meat and give it to Conor or Ralin, just as Baratho did when you were a child. You will make sure that the oldest ones have what they need, and that the youngest ones learn to hunt, sing the chants, and make tools. You will tell them of Baratho's kindness and honor, his sense of humor, and his wisdom. Through all of us, it will be as if he never left, for his spirit will be part of us and everything we do."

For the first time since returning from the hunt and learning of the tragedy, Griffo smiled.

"He made me work for the meat," said Griffo. "I had to walk to him when I was old enough, and sometimes he made me cut the meat myself. I had to name the animal from which it came and thank it for the sustenance it gave me. I felt pride when I did what he asked, even if he had to prompt me. I had not thought of him in that way for years,"

As they chatted, they caught up with Lura and Vica. The children of Vica were walking glumly beside their mother. Lura's father, Alek, had perished while keeping them and the clan safe from harm. The girls had lived with him just a short time, but he was the most important male in their life. Alek had made a home for them and had given them their happiest days.

Griffo put his arms over the girls' shoulders. He remembered almost nothing of his parents, who had died when he was young. In a way, he was fortunate to be of the age where memories, both good and bad, are not retained. Leeza had taken him in, and she was his mother in every way. He knew, however, that the girls must be suffering more than most.

"What did you give to Alek?" he asked. He was sure they must have left something that was meaningful to them.

Tali answered at once. "The knife we made. He showed me how to chip it. I thought he would need it on his crossing to the spirit world. I can make another. He taught me well."

"And you?" he asked Dani.

Return of the Lion People

"A basket, but it is not finished. Leeza was helping me. It was to be a surprise for Alek." She thought for a moment. "I wonder if he will finish it himself? Will his spirit need it on the journey?"

"I am sure he will finish it," said Lartha. "Alek had many skills. On the day that Leeza taught us to make baskets, he learned very quickly. He is like your mother in many ways." She turned to Vica. "Alek was one of those who built my shelter. He did something clever. He insisted on smoothing the poles. He removed the bark with a tool that he made himself. After that, he used the tool to smooth the wood. He finished each of the poles by making a special mark so I would know which ones were his. I will show you his work."

As Lartha spoke, Griffo thought of what she had said to him and looked at the girls. They were no longer burdened by the loss of Alek and peppered her with questions about him. Lartha was right, Griffo decided. Those who passed would always be with them.

When they reached the camp, there was much to do to restore it to a livable condition. In a way, this was a good thing, because the clan would be distracted from the incidents of the past few days. Before they began the reconstruction, however, an urgent duty must be performed. A new leader of the clan must be chosen.

In some clans, leaders were often determined by fighting ability, while in others there was family succession. The Wolf Clan, because of its history, depended on a different method. Succession had been based on family ties in the past, the problems with the sons of Ushga led to a change. A group of elders, most of them men, made the decision with the advice of Lartha. This system had been used to select Baratho, and it had proven to be successful. Baratho's sons would be in line for the position, as would many of the other men.

Those who would decide on the new leader sat in a circle in the middle of the camp. Their discussion was open to all, and on this day, not a single clan member was missing (except those abducted by the Lion People). Recent occurrences had united the clan in a way that was hard to describe, as adversity sometimes does, and they all wanted to be part of the process.

Matan, the oldest son of Baratho began the proceedings. He volunteered himself for the position, admitting to a sense of duty to carry on his father's legacy. He did so with the support of his two brothers. He then added something unexpected. "I would also like you to consider Zibio, my father's friend. For years, he has been steadfast and capable. In many ways, despite having a family of his own, he has been like a second father to us."

Maddia, who stood behind her father, was touched by this tribute to him. She thought of all he had done for her and the clan, especially for his support of her as she brought the wolves into the clan. Hearing her father proposed as a leader came as a complete surprise. In her memory, just one person, Baratho, had led the clan and her father was as loyal to him as a person could be.

Both of his brothers echoed Matan's sentiments. They spoke highly of Zibio and reminded those assembled of the events surrounding the coming of Nasha, the wolf, to the clan. Despite his daughter being responsible for adopting the wolf, Zibio not once entered the discussion to persuade Baratho, even though he was dedicated to his daughter and the wolf pup.

The pool of potential leaders was small. There were simply not that many mature men with the skills and experience to lead the clan. Such men were usually in the forefront during the hunt and when the clan was attacked. They were more likely to die than others. Matan was quick to admit that his youth made him less prepared for the position than Zibio.

The selection of Zibio as the leader did not take long. The small group of candidates, the words of Matan, and the counsel of Lartha made the outcome inevitable. Zibio accepted with humility. He showed gratitude to the sons of Baratho, understanding that their support so soon after the loss of their father must have been difficult despite their relationship. In fact, the entire clan was relieved that the change of leadership had gone so smoothly, knowing that in other tribes, there was often a period of violence and unrest upon the passing of a leader.

While the clan was together, Zibio took the opportunity to address them. His words described the three most pressing challenges that lay ahead. They must rebuild the village, hunt and gather the food they needed, and plan a rescue mission for those who had been captured by the Lion People.

A group of young people under the direction of Griffo and Maddia left for a hunt. Some of the women accompanied them, as did Nasha and Albo. They would look for small animals near camp. Through a series of sentinels, they would never be out of touch with those who remained in the village. The memory of the Lion People was still fresh in their minds.

A second group began rebuilding the shelters. They started with the ones that would be most easily repaired, because the clan would be sharing huts for days. Restoring the least damaged homes was the most efficient way to provide shelter for the greatest number of people.

The discussion of a rescue mission would have to be put off for a time. As eager as they were to get on with it, they recognized that they needed a plan and information. No one had any idea where the Lion People had their stronghold. Although they and the captives could be tracked easily, without knowledge of the layout of the camp itself, there was no way to develop a sensible rescue strategy.

Chapter 16

The women and children captives knew better than to resist. They had no weapons and were not trained as fighters. They did exactly as they were told.

The guards were not gentle when they bound the hands of the women and children. They left enough slack in the bindings so the captives could bear the objects stolen from the camp. Some of the warriors seemed to take pleasure in the pain the prisoners experienced when they were tied.

"Your fathers and brothers are cowards," said Dikach. "If they were brave, they would have protected you."

Salora, the oldest of the girls, muttered, "You will be sorry for what you have done." She glared at the man fearlessly. Neither of them understood the other because their languages were different.

The red-haired girl's mother quickly put her hand over the girl's mouth to keep her from saying anything. It was too late. Dikach had heard her. His reaction, however, was surprising.

"You are a feisty one," he hissed. "Maybe we will make a warrior woman out of you." Looking at her mother, he added, "You will not be around to watch over her. Is this other one yours, too?"

Ducatha pulled her other daughter, Reesa, to her side, and looked apologetic. She had no clue what he was saying, but everything about him made her skin crawl.

When Okar did not return, Dikach left to look for him. Ducatha was relieved, and she told the girls to be silent. She, like the others, was confused when Dikach came back screaming. They carried whatever the men gave them and were hurried away.

"What happened?" she whispered to Murra, another of the women. The mother of Murra was from another clan, and Murra had learned two languages as a child.

"I am not sure. I could understand only a few words. Okar is dead. He blames Lartha."

The members of the Wolf Clan who heard Murra's words were slightly uplifted. If Lartha had somehow killed Okar, then there was hope for them. This faint possibility of rescue helped to keep them alive during the next days.

The captives marched until sunset without food, water, or a rest. By mid-afternoon, they were suffering from the heat. The Lion People had their own food. They even carried water in bags made from animal skins and such. For them, the day was not much different from any other day.

The long march of the women and children was the most difficult any of them had undertaken. Fortunately, they only had to walk for half a day. They survived because they supported one another. The women with young children often had to carry both the looted objects given to them by the guards and their children. Some of the other women and the bigger children came to their aid. Hardly any captives had seed cakes or dried meat, but those who did shared what they had with others.

When the sun was about to touch the horizon, Dikach ordered them to stop. There was a treeless patch beside the river. He said to the captives in their own language, "We will camp here for the night. You may forage for food where the forest meets the clearing or in the river. You must stay bound together. When night falls, all of you must assemble in the center of the clearing."

At once, all of the captives headed for the river. The mothers had a hard time preventing the children from drinking too much at once. And as tired as they were, they had no time to rest. They had to gather food before dark. Dikach added to their burden. He insisted that they find wood for the fire.

"We cannot continue like this," sighed Murra. "None of us will survive." Her concern was justified. If the next days were as fatiguing as today, many of the women and children would die.

"Yes we will," answered Ducatha. "All of us will survive. We must put away food for tonight and tomorrow. We may not get to search for food in the morning. What is more important, we must have at least a little water with us."

Ducatha's words were somewhat reassuring to Murra and the other women who heard them. They picked edible leaves and fruit. Along the bank of the river they were able to catch small fish with their hands. Some of the older children found shellfish.

"Bring them all back to the fire," shouted Dikach to the guards. It was getting dark, and he did not want any of the captives to have an opportunity to hide.

"We have nothing to hold water," sighed Murra. "That will make tomorrow a very difficult day."

"The fruit we collect will have to get us through the day," answered Ducatha. "Try to save as much as you can for tomorrow. Tell the other women to do the same."

All of the captives were held in one place near the great fire. They ate the food they had found without cooking it. The guards took some of their the food the captives had gathered, so they had plenty to eat. The Lion People had also killed a boar and were roasting it. The smell of the meat cooking made the women and children even hungrier. The raw food they had eaten did little to satisfy them.

Luckily, the evening was not very cool. They snuggled up to one another and stayed as close to the fire as they could. The only good thing to come of their brutal day was exhaustion. All of them slept soundly through the night.

"All of you, wake up," shouted the guard. He and another warrior woke the sleepers in the morning with nudges and kicks. "We have no time to waste."

Almost at once, they were forced into marching. It was a struggle for all of them, particularly the children, who were not quite awake. Worst of all, they were sore from the trek of the day before.

As they set out, Murra said to Ducatha, "You were right about collecting extra food. I would not have thought of that."

Murra's daughter, Evalen, pointed to the sky. Clouds were beginning to build. "It is going to rain," she said sadly. "That will make things worse."

"The rain will make it better," said her mother, who tried to cheer her up. "We will not be as hot as yesterday, and we will have water to drink. Rain would be a good thing."

Before long, the rain started. It was uncomfortable, and they were now tired, cold, and wet. As the day wore on, however, things got better. They were no longer too hot, the rain kept them cool, and they had plenty of water to drink.

As they passed through a clearing, Murra spotted plants with gourds growing on them. Some of the gourds were large and were from the previous season.

"Grab a gourd," she said to her children, Noelo and Evalen. "We can use them to hold water."

She turned to Ducatha to tell her, but her friend and her children were already doing the same thing. The other women understood and picked gourds themselves.

"These gourds are from last season," Murra told her children. "We can clean out the insides. If we are careful not to puncture the outside, they will hold water."

The first challenge was to remove the top of the gourd. They had no cutting tools, as the guards had examined them to be sure no one had a weapon. Ducatha, however, had a necklace with a single shell. She took it off and cracked the shell against a rock. The edge was now sharp enough to cut the top from a gourd.

After cutting her gourd, she did the same for her daughters' gourds. She handed the shell to Murra and said in a quiet voice, "Do not let any of the guards see it."

The shell passed from woman to woman and eventually back to Ducatha. She put the necklace around her neck as before. The shell was too valuable a tool to leave behind. She hoped none of the guards noticed the sharp edge.

Murra picked up a stick and showed her

children how to scoop out the inside. "Be very gentle," she advised them, knowing how impatient Noelo was. "Remove the dried seeds and pulp carefully. Do not throw the seeds away. They are not very tasty, but we may have to eat them later."

The guards saw what they were doing. They did not, however, interfere. They let them persist not out of kindness, but because they knew that the journey would be difficult. They wanted their future slaves to be in good condition when they got back to their stronghold.

At midday, they stopped briefly. The captives were allowed to find what they could to eat. The women filled the gourds with water from a nearby stream. In addition, they stuffed leaves into the top of the gourds to hold the water inside. Both the leaves and the inside of the gourd would make the water taste bad, but it was better than nothing.

"We need a way to carry the gourds," said Ducatha to Murra. "With our hands bound and the burdens we have, it will be a struggle to manage one more thing."

"What about this?" suggested Salora. "We can tie a vine to a gourd and hang it over a shoulder. We can do it without using our hands. Even the little ones can do it." She pointed to her mother's necklace. "It would be like the shell around your neck."

"Very clever," said Ducatha to her daughter. "We can try it."

It took only a moment to cut a vine with the

shell, wrap it around a gourd, and tie it into a loop. Ducatha cut enough pieces of vine for the others, and by the time they set out again, all of them had gourds hanging from their shoulders.

Because she knew a little of the language of the Lion People, Murra was able to talk to one of the guards. He was not friendly, but he was willing to answer her questions.

"What happened to your other leader?" she asked. "I have forgotten his name."

"His name is Okar, and he is dead. Your sorceress killed him. We do not know what happened. Dikach would not go near the body. He said it was floating in the air."

Not wanting to anger him, Murra changed the topic. "Where are you taking us?"

The guard said nothing, and Murra did not ask twice. Eventually, he responded.

"You will come to our stronghold. It is still four days away. There are other captives there. You will have plenty of company."

"You will not harm us or the children?" Murra's words were more a plea than a question.

"That depends on you," the guard answered. "You are more valuable alive than dead. Our life is easier because of you. There is no need for us to seek food. You will do that for us. The same is true of other chores like fetching water or bringing in firewood."

"Did slaves build your camp?"

The guard scowled at Murra. "We took the

camp from the cliff dwellers. For years, we traveled toward the rising sun. We conquered many clans until we reached a desert. It was pointless to proceed. We turned and came back through a different route. The cliff dwellers had the perfect home for us. It is like a fortress. Needless to say, we took it from them. None of them are left. You will see why it is the right place for us...and soon enough, for you."

Murra told the others what she had learned. She was not sure she understood everything, but she had grasped enough.

They pressed on for a few more days. With the food they were able to find and the gourds to hold water, they all survived. When they arrived at their destination, they were not prepared for what they saw. The home of the Lion People was impregnable. An attack would never succeed. The chances of being rescued seemed very small.

Chapter 17

"Vica can help plan the rescue," said Lura. "She knows the layout of the place where the Lion People are living. I think she can show us where it is located."

Zibio and the others were assembled around the fire. The morning was chilly, and because of the warmth of the fire, they were comfortable. They were talking about how they should proceed with the rescue of the captives.

"When can we start?" asked Griffo, jumping to his feet. He was not yet a man, but Griffo was gallant and loyal to the clan. He was having a difficult time not doing something about the missing women and children.

"We know how eager you are," said Zibio, "but we must proceed with caution. We do not want to endanger our people. I am not sure we should attempt a rescue until they are in the camp of the Lion People."

"And why not?" demanded Griffo.

"Any effort to save them while they are traveling puts us and the captives at a disadvantage. They would most likely be victims at the hands of the Lion People. Our own people might even hurt them. I know how hard this is on you, but I think it is better to wait until they get to the camp." Zibio spoke softly, realizing that Griffo had good intentions, but that his thinking was not clear in this situation.

Griffo looked as if he was going to shout something, but instead sat down. "I am sorry for speaking so loudly. You are right, and I know it. I do not like being in this situation where our people are in danger, especially the children. If we are to save them, we need a sensible plan. You can count on me not to do anything rash."

"We are going to rescue them," said Maddia, and she walked over to Griffo. He had spent much time with the children who had been taken captive, often caring for them when their parents were hunting or gathering. Even now, as the tallest member of the clan and a skilled hunter, he had great affection for the children.

Maddia sat beside him, as did Nasha. Griffo could not resist petting Nasha when she put her head in his lap. As she often did, Nasha sensed that one of her people needed consolation. She was able to give Griffo the comfort that would improve his spirits.

"Vica, do you know where the stronghold is?"

asked Fong.

Vica signaled that she knew where it was, but she made a facial expression that showed she was somewhat uncertain. Because she was not familiar with the region, she was able to represent only the most obvious features of the terrain. She got a stick and moved to a sandy piece of ground between the group and the fire. She drew a map showing what she remembered from her escape.

The encampment of the Lion People was beside a large body of water from which flowed a river. The camp was beside a cliff that was part of a long range of low mountains. Beyond the mountain range was a mix of forest and grassland. The final place she drew was where she had encountered the lion and met the clan.

As Vica drew her map, Fong recognized the stronghold of the Lion People and explained to the others what he knew. "They have taken over another clan's camp. I passed through it after my people died, and I had to find a new clan. The cliff people there were friendly. They fished in the great sea for much of their food." He added thoughtfully, "It will be difficult getting to the encampment. The sea is on one side, and a near-vertical cliff is on the other. There are only two trails leading into the camp, and they can be defended easily."

"You have given us a good idea where the camp is. Can you draw a map of the stronghold itself?" asked Zibio.

Vica had only a vague idea of where the camp was; however, she knew the inside well. The map she drew was highly detailed and showed that the captives at one end of the camp where they could be easily guarded. The rest of the camp was close to a steep cliff. The shelters of the Lion People were built against the side of the cliff. Some of the warriors lived in caves in the cliff itself.

"That is as much as I know," added Fong. "Some of the caves were fairly deep, while others were just crevices in the cliff. Like the paths that lead in, the stronghold could be defended very easily. I do not think we can come at them directly and hope to succeed."

Vica nodded in agreement. She showed how she and the girls got away. They and some others had been picking fruit. They were well guarded, but they were working at the edge of the forest. The three of them had gone into the forest and returned with fruit and edible leaves several times. On the last trip, rather than heading into the jungle, they scrambled up the cliff part of the way back to the stronghold and waited.

Their strategy was easy to understand. They believed that their absence would not be detected. If it was, and they were spotted by the guards, they could say they were not running off but were lost. They were hoping to make their way back to camp along the ridge.

Lura added some details that Vica had shared with her and that she thought would be useful to the others. "When the work was finished, the guards marched the prisoners to the stronghold. They walked behind the captives. They thought that no one could get away because the path went between the cliff and the sea, so no one could have gotten past them."

"What did they do next?" asked Tulio.

"They waited until the sun had set and then ran along the trail away from the stronghold. Vica was not sure where they were going. They noted where the sun set and went in that direction. That night, they found a small cave. They stacked stones in front of the opening to keep animals out. Before dawn, they left the cave and set off toward the mountain behind which the sun had set. They would take periodic breaks and withdraw from the trail to see if they were being followed. None of the Lion People were on their trail, so they kept going. At night, they either climbed trees or stayed in caves. They traveled for five days until they found the mammoth carcass."

"That means it will take us three or four days to get to the stronghold of the Lion People," said Fong. "We know the terrain better than Vica did and can probably move faster."

"We will be hampered by the food that we will have to carry because we will not be able to do too much hunting. We will have to be stealthy and stay hidden," remarked Zibio. "A group of our size would certainly be noticed by the Lion People if we stayed on the main trail."

"How many of us will be needed for the rescue attempt?" asked Griffo.

No one had an answer. It was a question they had not asked to this point. When they thought about it, the difficulty of the task became more evident. There were about twenty members of the clan who could be reasonably expected to travel so far and fight if it became necessary. Half of these would have to be left at the camp for defense. That means only ten or so people could go on the rescue. The mission seemed more and more impossible.

"Our problem is not too many, but too few," commented Zibio. "Only ten of us can participate in the rescue. I cannot imagine how we will defeat the Lion People with such a small force."

"We do not have to defeat them," said Griffo, "just get the captives out without being discovered. We can do it."

The confidence with which Griffo spoke had a positive effect on the rest of the group. They faced an enormous challenge, but they felt they could achieve their goal. The most critical factor would be avoiding detection, as Vica and the girls had done.

"The simplest plan has the best probability of success," advised Lartha. "There are not as many things that can go wrong. And Griffo has described our purpose clearly. We do not want to engage the Lion People. We just want to get the captives out."

"Will we try to save just our people?" asked Lakus.

"I am not sure we can do that," counseled Zibio, "and I do not think it is wise. Our plan should include all the captives who want to be free. We should not force anyone to go with us, but we should give them the opportunity."

"Then we must accept the possibility that some of the captives may actually alert the guards that something is going on," said Maddia.

"That is not very likely," signed Vica. "No one that would choose to stay if they had an option. Some may fear getting caught, but I believe they would simply say nothing and stay."

"Our plan is becoming clear," said Tulio. "We must make our way to the stronghold of the Lion People without being seen. I am guessing that we will wait until nightfall. When most of the Lion People are asleep, we shall lead the captives from the camp. We can flee with them, hoping that we will have most of a night to travel before they know what happened."

"That is a good description of what we must accomplish," said Zibio. "For the beginning of the getaway, we must stay together. Once the sun rises, it may make sense for us to disperse into groups. If we stay together, we will be easier to locate."

"How many captives are there?" asked Fong.

"They took more than twenty of our people," answered Zibio. "Vica, how many more are there?"

Vica did not answer at once. She drew an outline on the ground. In it, she drew marks to indicate the individuals in the groups that were in the cave where the captives were held. There were more than a hundred captives, which was more than the clan itself. Vica's indication of the number of captives showed that the rescue would be more complicated than anyone had imagined. At the same time, it became more critical because so many people were involved.

"The plan must be accomplished in two parts," said Fong. "The initial task is to get the captives as far away as we can. When morning comes, we must press on. If there is water on the way, we should drink, but we cannot stop for any length of time. Only when the sun is high should we disperse into small groups and forage for food and water. For the rest of the day, we should hide. The warriors of the Lion People will be moving faster than we are, and they will be getting close. By remaining out of sight, we will reduce our chances of being found. When it is dark, we can continue on our journey."

"We will need a meeting place after the first day," said Maddia. "If we separate into groups, we may not be able to locate one another. At least one of us should stay with each group of captives so we can direct them back to our camp. Is there a place that we can meet at dusk?"

"I would never have considered that," said Zibio to his daughter. "It is a good thing that you mentioned the need for a meeting place. Does anyone have any ideas?"

"The hill with the flat top can be seen from a distance. That would be a good place to meet," recommended Fong.

"It is ideal," said Vica. "We went by there. A spring is on the sunset side of the hill. It flows into a creek. We drank the water and found some fruit. Fish were in the creek, but we had no time to catch them."

"We will meet at dusk near the spring on the sunset side of the hill with the flat top," said Zibio. "Whoever gets there will stay until it is dark and then go on through the night. If any of the groups are not there, they should head back to our camp. Although it will take longer, we should probably follow the river."

"That is logical," said Griffo. "It will take more time, but it will be better because of the protection offered by the forest near the river. The Lion People will probably track us along the main trail and will assume that we will stay on that path."

"If we all follow the river, we will eventually meet if we are separated," added Maddia. "It is also the best way to reach our camp for people who do not know the area. The camp can be seen from the ridge beside the river."

"There is one more thing we must be prepared for," said Zibio. "The Lion People will be inclined to attack us later after they discover what happened. We may have to abandon our village and move."

No one said a word in response to Zibio. What he was suggesting was an outcome none of them wished for, but they knew it might happen. Even if the rescue was successful, they may have to leave their home forever.

Chapter 18

On the morning after the meeting, the young people of the clan went to the stream near the camp. They had no special purpose; they just wanted to be with one another. The events of the past days had been overwhelming for them.

"What do you think of the plan?" Piero asked.

His brother, Ganni, answered quickly. "I do not like it. There are too many things that can go wrong. I did not comment at the meeting because I have no better alternative. I must trust what the others say."

"The plan we have decided on lets us get started quickly. That is the most important element," argued Griffo.

Maddia said nothing, but she listened carefully to the others. She stroked Nasha, who lay quietly beside her. Albo rested a little ways off, as he usually did. Even though they were near the camp, Albo still acted as a sentinel. He knew that his duty was to look after his pack.

"My concern is that the rescuers will be seen as they approach the camp of the Lion People," said Katia. "Even though I will not be among them, I am worried. With only ten rescuers, there is no way that they could safeguard themselves from the Lion People."

"Is there not another path that leads to the camp of the Lion People?" asked Maddia. "The riskiest phase seems to be getting into the stronghold. Leaving the camp, or even fleeing, is less worrisome."

"If we traveled by night, we would be less likely to be seen," added Lakus. "The trip would take longer because we would have to move more slowly."

His brother, Tulio, said something that got their attention. "We are thinking about the rescue in the wrong way. Is there not another way we can get to the camp of the Lion People? What if we went around the stronghold and came in from the side? Could we not climb down the cliff?"

Without thinking, Piero blurted out, "The sea... we could cross the sea in rafts!"

"That is ridiculous," said Griffo. He thought for a moment and then added uncertainly, "Maybe not." He was suddenly intrigued by what Piero had said.

"How wide is the sea near their camp?" asked Lakus.

"We can ask Vica to be sure, but think about

her map," said Tulio. "The camp was not far from where the river came out. That is not the widest part of the sea. And we do not have to cross the whole sea. We can build rafts away from the camp and float to the beach at night. If we are noticed, we do not have to land. How could the Lion People catch us if we were on rafts in the water?"

"I know how to build rafts," said Piero. "Come with me, and I will show you."

Piero ran beside the stream and around a bend to where it broadened. There on the bank of the stream was a raft like the one they had seen while returning to camp after the mammoth hunt. It was smaller, but in every other way, it was the same.

"When did you build this?" asked Maddia.

"The day after we saw the raft," answered Piero. "Whenever I had time, I did a little more. Putting the raft together did not take that long, and it was not that strenuous. Most of the time went into cutting the logs and finding the vines to hold everything together."

With that, Piero pushed the raft into the stream. He picked up a long pole and got onto the raft. He pushed off from the bank and into the stream. The current was weak, but it caused him to drift downstream steadily. He floated for a short distance and then began to pole upstream. He passed the others, drifted back down, and floated to the bank.

"We will only need two rafts," he said. "They will be bigger than this, but not by much. A raft that size can easily hold five people and a wolf."

"What happens if the raft turns over in a storm or we fall off?" asked Lakus.

"We can swim," said Tulio. "If you do not know how to swim, we will teach you. We learned from Nasha. You can learn, too. You will not have to swim for long. A raft cannot sink."

"But we will have to carry the rafts for days," said Griffo. "We can do it, but it will be grueling."

Piero said, "I did not think about that." He seemed a little disappointed in himself.

"But we do not have to bring the rafts," said Maddia. "There are trees we can use by the great sea. There might even be enough vines growing there, but we can take some vines with us. We will need some tools, but they can serve as weapons. How long will it take ten of us to build two rafts?"

"About a day," answered Piero. "The work is not demanding."

"Will the wolves be able to go on the raft?" asked Maddia.

"I have no idea," said Piero. "We can try it now. Sit on the raft with me, Maddia. We can see if Nasha will come to us."

The raft was resting on the bank of the river. Part of it was in the water. Piero and Maddia clambered onto the raft and sat down. Maddia called Nasha, who came right over. She sniffed at the raft and then climbed onto it. She had no fear at all and sat down beside Maddia.

"What about Albo?" asked Ganni. "He has

always been more cautious than Nasha.

There was no more room on the small raft, so Piero got off. He and the others backed away from the raft. Maddia beckoned to Albo, who walked over to her. Like Nasha, he sniffed the raft, but unlike her, he did not get on it at once. He paced back and forth whining slightly. Maddia was patient and kept calling him with a soft voice. He stepped onto the raft, licked her face, and lay down beside her.

"We will have to practice a few times, I think," she said, "and we will have to push the raft into the river. I think they will be fine. The wolves are good swimmers and are not afraid of the water."

Maddia did not get up at once. She wanted the wolves to spend time on the raft while they finished talking about the plan. Both of them settled into a comfortable position. Nasha lay on her side and napped. Albo put his head on his paws but did not sleep. As he did before, he watched over those around him.

"What do you think the others will think of the plan?" asked Ganni. "It is very different from what we agreed to."

"No one was completely satisfied with the plan as it is. I think they would be willing to talk about what Piero has proposed and evaluate his notion fairly," said Tulio.

"Then we should discuss Piero's plan with Zibio and the others," said Ganni. "I have confidence that they will listen."

Return of the Lion People

They left the stream and found Zibio with Fong. Piero explained his plan briefly. Zibio expressed his doubts.

"We have no experience building rafts, and we are not even sure if we can reach the camp by water," he argued. "But I have to admit that there are risks with the plan that we have."

"Maddia, will you please track down Vica and Lura? We should tell the others who are going with us. I think they should hear what you are suggesting. Vica will be especially helpful because she knows the terrain around the camp of the Lion People," added Fong.

It was not long before all of those involved in the rescue came together. Piero described his plan, and once again, those who heard it were filled with questions. No one, however dismissed what he was saying. As they discussed the plan, they began to see its possibilities.

Zibio turned to Vica and asked one of the most important questions. "Is there a place near the stronghold of the Lion People to make the rafts without being seen?"

After thinking for a moment, Vica made a map on the ground. It showed the camp of the Lion People beside the sea. She drew the place where the river flowed out of the sea. On the far side of the river, the shore of the sea was in a crescent shape. If trees grew there, the site would not be visible from the camp.

"I know that place," said Fong. "It could not be

better. There are low hills that go down to the water. The forest is thick. It is hard to get to the spot because the river is wide there. We will have to cross the river well below the camp. After that, we will have to walk along the shore. I do not know if a trail is there, so it may be difficult."

"You sound as if you have more faith in the raft plan," said Zibio.

Fong hesitated and then answered, "The task is more or less unworkable. A small number of us will be going against many. We are hunters. They are warriors. We will be away from home. They have every advantage except one. We are smarter than they are. They will never expect us to come by the water. In addition, with Piero's plan, we have an escape route if we are discovered. I cannot imagine that they have rafts that could catch us."

All eyes turned to Zibio. As the leader of the clan, he would have the final decision. He looked around at those gathered before him. They included his children and his best friends. The course of action he chose would put them all in danger, yet it might result in the rescue of those they loved.

"Let me think about what you have proposed," he said. "And I would like all of you to think about it too. I have found that we often make better choices if we come back to them after a time." He then added, "If we do follow Piero's plan, we will have to know how to build rafts. We should probably get started with that immediately. It will be a good skill for us to know."

Hearing Zibio's suggestion, the young people all smiled and looked at one another. They thought that what he said made sense. They felt that he had shown respect for a proposal put forth by one of their friends. Zibio's saying that they should learn to build rafts implied that he was favoring Piero's plan. Maddia gave Piero a hug, which embarrassed him to no end. His brother, Ganni, punched him in the arm as a sign of affection.

"There is one more thing," said Piero in a quiet voice. "All of those who do not know how to swim should learn. As Lakus has pointed out, if a raft turns over or one of us tumbles off, we will have to know how to swim."

"We can do that today," said Griffo. "Maddia, Tulio, and Katia taught me how to swim last year. It did not take long, and it was fun. Nasha and Albo swam with us. Who does not know how to swim?"

All the young people present knew how to swim. It was the adults who did not. They all had excuses about why they could not learn right now, but the young people insisted. The group went to the stream near camp where the water slowed and formed a pool. In the middle of the pool, the water was deep enough to swim, but not so deep as to be hazardous.

Maddia and Katia walked into the water with the wolves. When the water came up to their waists, they began to swim. The style of the girls' swimming was like that of the wolves. They paddled around in a circle with their heads above water.

"Who wants to try it?" asked Katia.

None of the adults wanted to be first, which made the young people grin. After a moment, Lura and Vica stepped into the water. They looked fearful, but they grinned.

"I will be right behind you," said Tulio. "The depth of the water is not great, and you will be able to stand up at any time. Watch Nasha for a moment. See how she paddles with her front and back paws. Look at Katia. She is moving steadily, and her head stays above the water."

Vica walked to the wolves and girls. She leaned forward and paddled tentatively. Lura was right behind her. Both of them felt anxious as the water crept up to their faces, but they did not stop paddling, nor did they panic. They moved closer to the wolves, looked at each other, and giggled.

"I have not felt like that since I was a girl," said Lura. "I cannot describe the sensation. It is like I am dreaming about flying."

"That is how we felt," said Tulio, who was ready to come to their aid if it was necessary.

The two women paddled back to shallow water and stood up. They and the young people looked at Zibio, Fong, and the other men. Laughing, they began the challenge chant. This was a children's song that they used to dare one another to do silly things, like climb a tree or jump from rock to rock. The men joined in the laughter and accepted the challenge. They walked into the deeper water, and after a little thrashing, began to paddle like the wolves.

"It is not as easy as it looks," said Zibio. "All of us who are new swimmers will need practice. Even if we become capable swimmers, I would prefer that we never have to use this new skill on the rescue."

Two nights later at the community fire, Zibio discussed Piero's plan with the whole clan. By then, they knew what was going on, but this was an opportunity to talk about it as a group. No one was surprised at the opinion Zibio expressed.

"I have evaluated the idea of the raft and listened to all of you. I think the plan is a good one. The time is near when we can attempt a rescue."

Chapter 19

The captured women and children scaled a hill beside a river. From the top of the hill, they could see the great sea. In the distance was a rocky cliff. At the base of the cliff was the stronghold of the Lion People.

Ducatha looked at the sea. She sighed and said, "Such a beautiful view. In another time, we might remember this day happily."

"Some day we shall be happy again," said Salora. "I know it."

Salora held her sister Reesa's hand. They were bound together and tied to their mother, but she still held her sister's hand. She pointed out some birds flying along the shore. Ducatha smiled at Salora's effort to make the horrible journey as pleasant as possible for her sister.

They descended the hill, and by late in the afternoon, they reached the camp of the Lion People. The captives were forced into a cave that was filled with others who had been captured by the Lion People.

"This is where you will stay," said Dikach. "Do not hope for rescue."

The words of Dikach were easy to believe. The stronghold of the Lion People seemed invulnerable. It was built into the side of a cliff that was immediately beside the water. There were only two ways to approach the camp, and both were well-defended. The captives realized that there was a good chance they would be here for the rest of their lives.

As the guards drove the new captives into the cave, those inside huddled against the walls. They said nothing and did not even look at the newcomers while the guards were inside. The guards cut the bindings so the new captives could move around more freely. The members of the Wolf Clan clustered near the entrance of the cave. They were afraid and confused.

When the guards withdrew, things changed. Whispers from the back of the cave called them. Some were in unfamiliar languages. Others they understood. They walked to the shadows at the back of the cave, not knowing what to expect.

"You must be hungry," they heard someone say. "We have extra food. Come and sit near us. Do not say anything or the guards will come."

Murra led her children toward the voices, and the others followed. They sat near a small group of captives. Small pieces of fruit, dried meat, and seed cake were handed to them. Not a word was spoken by anyone, and they ate the food silently.

"We save what food we can," said a young man. "My name is Han. There is a spring at the far side of the cave if you need water."

"Our village was attacked by the Lion People," said Ducatha. "We do not know what happened to the rest of our people."

"All of us came here the same way," said Han. "Some of us saw our villages destroyed and our people killed. We have been in this place for almost a year. Before that, we moved from place to place. When the Lion People found a village they liked, they did not destroy it. They stayed in the village until they decided to move on. I think they like this place best of all."

"How long have you been with the Lion People?" asked Murra.

"I am not sure," answered Han. "Many years. They stole me from my family when I was just a boy. Others have been here for a long time, too. I was lucky to be young when they came. They killed all the older boys and men in my village."

Han's words were disturbing. Murra, Ducatha, and the others had not seen the hunting party return. They had heard the sounds of a battle, but it had been short. They did not know what had happened to the oldest clan members or the women with very young children.

"Where will we sleep?" asked Reesa. She looked at Ducatha and then at Han.

"We sleep here," said Han. "It is not very pleasant. The Lion People will not let us have animal skins. We gather leaves and bring them back each day. We can help you collect leaves tomorrow. It will take a while until you have enough for a sleeping place. In the meantime, you can crowd in beside us. Luckily, it is not very cold. In the winter, sleeping is a problem. We have only a small fire because we are afraid of the bedding catching fire."

Han sounded apologetic. He had told this story to other captives, and he knew how hard it was for them to adjust to life with the Lion People.

"Thank you for sharing your sleeping area," said Ducatha. "All of us are so tired that for tonight, at least, we will sleep well."

When the new captives woke the next morning, they found that the other prisoners were already up and around. They were preparing for the work that the Lion People expected them to do. There was little to eat because they had shared their food the night before.

"You will probably come with us to pick fruit today," said Han. "There is plenty of food this time of year, and you will be able to eat while you harvest. Be sure to hide some food and bring it back with you."

A woman standing nearby looked at Han. The man shook his head and looked away. The woman came up to Ducatha and pulled her aside.

"My name is Maril. I am sorry about what I

must tell you. Han was not at ease saying this." She hesitated and then continued. "The Lion People will not let the children go with you. They know that you will not try to escape if your children are here."

Ducatha turned quickly and looked at her two girls and the other children. She tried to calm herself. She did not want the children to see that she was upset.

"What can we do?" asked Ducatha.

"There is a little food we can leave with the children," said Maril. "We shall be gone from morning until late in the day. They will be safe here. The Lion People will not harm them. They know that they will control you through the children. They also realize that the children will grow up to be slaves. If the Lion People can bond with the children, they will be more willing to do as they are told."

"What do you mean?" asked Murra. She had come over to hear what Maril was saying.

"You will see some slaves in the camp. They wander about without restrictions. They are children who grew up in the camp. They have come to trust the Lion People. Because they are dependable, they receive more food and live in better conditions." Maril looked at the two women sadly, as if she had a secret she was hiding. "Do not hate them. It is not their fault. They were separated from their families and were lured into trusting the Lion People."

A noise at the front of the cave got their attention. Maril and Han quickly gave what little food they had to the children of the newcomers. As Maril had predicted, the Lion People separated the women from the children. All of the adults, who were mostly women, were led from the cave. Ducatha turned to her daughters and said, "Take care of the others."

Salora and Reesa had taken care of young children before. They knew exactly what to do. The two of them herded the children to the spring. They divided the food among the children and brought the youngest ones over to get water. Salora distracted the children with some games that used small sticks and rocks. When she saw some drawings on the cave wall, she pointed them out and began to tell stories.

"This is a mammoth," said Salora. "It is a huge animal. I saw some mammoths once. They ate the figs we picked. Let me tell you the story."

After Salora finished the story, one of the children got up and went to the wall of the cave. He pointed to a drawing of a wolf and said, "Look, it is Nasha." He said bravely, "Nasha and Albo will save us. I know they will."

A shadow fell across the wall meaning someone had come into the cave. All the children became quiet. Salora and Reesa put themselves between the children and the person who had entered the cave. They had nothing to protect themselves or the children.

"My name is Farad," said a boy. He was not much older than Salora. "My mother is Maril. She was in here with you. She is gathering with the others. I brought you some more food. I cannot stay, but remember me to my mother."

Farad put down an animal skin bag and ran off. Inside were some seed cakes, fruit, and dried meat. Before he left the cave, he said, "Do not forget to tell my mother that I was here."

The appearance of the boy and the food he brought made everyone more cheery. Reesa handed out some of the food to the children, but not all of it. She thought that they would be alone for a long time, and they would need more food later. Salora told the children the story of the mammoths and the figs.

At the end of the day, the women were overjoyed to see the children. The children were just as pleased to see them, and they were in a surprisingly good mood. Salora and Reesa had done a good job of entertaining them, and they were well fed.

"Where did you get the food?" asked Ducatha.

"Farad brought it to us," said Salora. "We have to tell his mother he was here. Who is his mother?"

"I am," said Maril. "You said that Farad brought you food?"

"Yes, he brought enough food for all of us. He seemed very nice. He wanted us to be sure to tell you he was here."

Maril looked surprised, then she smiled. "I

Return of the Lion People

thought I had lost him to the Lion People."

"How could he be lost?" asked Murra.

"The Lion People took him from me years ago. They raised him as one of their own. He serves them, and he is being taught how to be a warrior. I was concerned that he had been turned away from us."

"He is not one of them," said Salora. "Even if he pretends to be."

The mothers were eager to spend time with their children, but before they did, they had two chores to perform. One was to put the soft leaves and grasses they had found in the sleeping place. The second was to put their food together with that carried by others.

While they had been working that day, the Wolf Clan people learned how the prisoners survived. All of them ate what they could during the day. When they returned to the cave, they put their food together, creating a supply that was shared. They first ate the food that might spoil, like fresh meat and some fruits. Seeds, nuts, and fruit that had been dried were saved for another time. They did not get much fish or meat, but when they did, they tried to dry some of it so it lasted for a long time. They sometimes ground up the seeds and baked small cakes by the fire. All of this was necessary because there was so little food available during the winter and early spring.

Before they slept that night, Ducatha asked Maril about her clan. She was stunned by what she learned from the woman.

"The leader of our clan is Valtar. He is also my husband, and Farad is our son. Farad and I were kidnapped while we were on the way to visit my sister. We were traveling with some others along the river that flowed from the great sea. The Lion People came upon us suddenly. The others were killed. I was spared because of Farad. As they did with you, they brought me back to their stronghold. I did not know it at the time, but they needed laborers. They had just taken over the camp by the sea. I have no idea what has happened to my clan or my husband."

"Valtar is alive, and your clan is fine," said Ducatha. "They did us a service us when we were in need. Valtar is a good friend of our clan and is esteemed by our people." Looking at Maril, Ducatha added something that she thought was important. "Valtar has no wife. We did not know why, because he is such a good man. Now I understand."

From that day onward, Maril became special to the Wolf Clan. So did her son, Farad, who brought the prisoners treats whenever he could. As difficult as the next days would be, they were made better because of Maril and Farad.

Chapter 20

Over the next several days, the group of rescuers practiced swimming until they were proficient. At the same time, they learned from Piero how to build rafts and how to use them. The process was not difficult, but they had to be able to work quickly and soundlessly to avoid detection.

The initial raft they built used logs that had been cut or were on the ground. They chose logs that were close to the same length. Near the end of each log, they cut a groove for the vines that would hold the logs together. One thing they discovered was that they needed a way to measure the distance from the end of the log to the groove.

"I used my hand," said Piero. "I put my fingers on the end of the log and marked where the bottom of my hand was."

"Do you think it will make much of a difference whose hand is used for the measurement?" asked Tulio.

"Probably not," answered Piero. "Our hands are about the same size, and the slight variations will mean only that the grooves will not be even."

"How about the depth of the groove for the vines?" asked Fong.

"The grooves have to be deeper than the vines," said Piero. "If they are not, the vines can be cut when the logs rub against one another. I do not know how long that will take, but I hope we do not find out. If the vines wear through while we are on the water, the rafts will fall apart."

The raft they made took more than a day. All of them had worked on it. That meant they would have to improve their speed considerably. For the plan to succeed, they thought they would have to make two rafts in one day.

On the way back to the camp, Piero walked with Fong and Tulio. They talked about the work they had accomplished. They were disappointed, but Fong believed they would get faster.

"There is one more problem," suggested Tulio. "Today we used logs that were cut or were on the ground. When we make the rafts for the rescue, we will probably have to cut some logs."

"That should not be any trouble," said Piero. "I have used an axe to cut logs for a raft."

"The problem is not cutting the logs, but the noise we will make. I am concerned that cutting logs may alert the Lion People. We will be cutting logs near the sea, and the sound may carry all the way to the camp of the Lion People. We do not know how far we will be from them."

Fong looked troubled. "This is not something that is resolved easily," he said. "We will have to talk about it with the others in the morning. Maybe the answer will come to us by tomorrow."

When Tulio arrived at his family's hut, all of them were waiting for him. Belia and Zibio were cooking the evening meal. Maddia and Lakus were cutting meat into thin strips. They would let it dry for a time so it would not spoil and could be used that winter. The wolves were gnawing on bones.

Tulio helped his parents with dinner. He wrapped root vegetables in leaves and put them between the fire and the rocks that surrounded it. While he did, he talked about cutting the logs for the rafts.

"Do you think we will come up with a solution?" asked Zibio. "There is a chance that the Lion People will not hear us, but I would be more optimistic if we made as little noise as possible."

"Beavers cut trees without making much noise," said Maddia. "They chew through the wood."

"We could try cutting the trees using knives the way that beavers use their teeth," said Lakus. "That might take a long time."

The wolves paid little attention to their humans and focused instead on the bones. Nasha had almost chewed through hers. With her paws, she repositioned it in her mouth.

"Look at how Nasha has gnawed into her bone," said Maddia. "And Albo, too. They do not seem to have any trouble cutting through a bone. Nor do they make much noise."

Tulio watched the strong jaws of the wolves cut through the bones. Something about what they did got him thinking. Their jaws were long and filled with sharp teeth. Their shape reminded him in a certain way of a knife. The blade of a knife was smooth, but the teeth in the jaws of a wolf were jagged.

"We can saw wood with the blade of a knife!" he said. "It would be like the jaws of a wolf cutting through a bone."

"But a knife blade will not cut wood very well," said Zibio. "It is too smooth."

"We can make the blade more jagged," said Tulio. "When we first make a knife, the blade is rough. We keep chipping away to make it smoother. Suppose we did not make it smooth. The knife might be able to saw through the wood like a wolf chews through a bone."

Although it was becoming dark, Tulio could not wait. He left the shelter and ran to Fong's place. The toolmaker was working at his outside hearth.

"Should you not be home eating your mother's cooking?" he asked.

"Yes, but Nasha and Albo gave me an idea. It will solve the cutting problem, at least I think it will. What if we did not smooth the edge of a long

Return of the Lion People

knife? The rough edge would be like a wolf's teeth. We could then move the blade back and forth and cut the wood more quietly. We would not have to strike the wood with an axe."

Fong understood at once what he meant. He looked over the tools he was making and chose a knife with a long blade. He had just started shaping it, so the blade was still rough. He put it in the fire for a while, and when it was hot, pulled it out using two sticks. Fong wrapped a piece of animal skin around the handle, which was too hot to touch. He placed the unfinished knife on a stone and hit it with another stone.

"Normally, I would hit the blade again and again to smooth it. For this blade, I will tap it with the striking stone in only a few places." He explained what he was doing to Tulio as he worked the stone.

With just a handful of taps on each side of the blade, Fong had made a rough edge with jagged teeth that looked like a wolf's. He frowned a little, because an edge like this on a knife was not usually adequate. He also resisted the temptation to smooth it.

"May I try to cut with it?" asked Tulio. He ran to the pile of wood near the hearth and grabbed a piece that was the thickness of his arm.

"Here, take the blade," said Fong, "but remember, it is hot. Hold the animal skin wrapped around the handle."

Tulio took the blade from Fong carefully, not

wanting to burn his hand. He looked at the blade and the piece of wood. He could not put the wood on the ground and cut it. There would be no way to move the blade back and forth.

"What do I do now?" he asked Fong. "I cannot drag the blade across the wood with any force. I did not think beyond using it with a tree, which stands upright in the ground."

"Then do what we ordinarily do with tools. Put the wood down on the stone. You can lean on the wood to hold it in place."

As Fong suggested, Tulio placed the piece of wood on the stone. Part of hit hung over both sides of the stone. He held the wood down with one hand and slid the blade of the jagged-edged knife over the wood. It made a cut into the wood. Tulio moved the blade back and forth steadily over the wood and formed a deep groove.

He cut about halfway through the wood and took a break. It was more tiring than he thought it would be. When he continued, he put his knee on the piece of wood as well as his hand. Tulio found this position let him saw more efficiently because his weight could hold the wood in place. He sawed with the blade until he was all the way through the wood.

"Your blade worked well," said Fong. "It is too dark to try it now, but tomorrow, we shall cut a standing tree. Now, go on back to your family before Lakus forgets he has a brother and eats your food. Be sure to show your father the new kind of blade."

On the following morning, when the group arrived at the place by the river, Fong was already there. He held two long knives that appeared to be unfinished.

"That is not like you," said Griffo, poking fun at his friend. "Your tools are flawless as a rule." Seeing the smile on Fong's face, he added, "There is something you are not telling us."

"I shall let Tulio tell you the story."

"Let me show them how it works while I talk," said the boy.

Tulio had the blade Fong gave him the night before, but he decided to try one of the other blades that Fong was holding. They were a little longer, and he could see that the teeth of these places were more evenly spaced. Fong must have stayed up most of the night to make them.

Tulio chose a tree that was as thick as his leg. This was a good size for the raft. He knelt down and sawed the blade back and forth.

"When I saw the wolves chewing a bone last night, a thought came to me. If we had a tool with jagged edges, we might be able to cut through trees noiselessly. I told Fong about it, and he made these tools."

No one said anything. They just watched him saw through the tree. The work was hard, but the blade worked well. Suddenly, however, Tulio stopped cutting. The tree had pinched the blade. Tulio could not move it.

"I should have thought of that," he said with frustration. "I cut in the wrong place. I should have started on the other side. The angle of the tree is important."

"We can fix that," said Griffo. He leaned against the tree and moved it enough for Tulio to pull the blade out.

With a few more strokes of the blade on the other side of the trunk, the tree fell. Tulio stood up with a look of satisfaction. He handed the blade to Griffo and told him to try it. Griffo seemed uncertain how to begin, so Tulio and Fong showed him what to do.

One after another, the others were given a chance to use the new tool. As each of them tried it, they developed new techniques to cut the trees and remove the limbs. When it came time to notch the logs for the vines, the new tool worked just as well.

"I shall make more of these cutting tools as soon as possible," said Fong. "The blade has worked better than either of us imagined. Not only is using it more quiet than cutting with an axe, but I think it cuts more quickly." Looking at the wolves resting nearby, he added, "Be sure to thank Nasha and Albo."

"We have three of the new tools," said Zibio. "We should probably spend the rest of the day practicing with them. The time is coming when we will attempt our rescue. The captives must be having a very difficult time."

Each day, the group got better at making rafts. They even spent time at the river building a raft and taking it into a larger body of water. These rehearsals gave all of them renewed confidence in the plan. Those who would participate in the rescue formed themselves into two teams. There was no room for error, and the better they worked together, the more likely it was they would be successful.

On the night of the full moon, Zibio gathered the clan around the fire. "It is time," he said. "Tomorrow we shall leave. It will take us four days or so to reach the place where we will build the rafts. There will be enough moonlight for us to execute our plan without being seen easily by the Lion People. This will be our last night together for some time. Let us make the most of it."

Chapter 21

The morning of the departure was gloomy. A light rain fell, and mist covered the village. Those who were in the rescue party said their goodbyes. None of them knew if they would see their home again. Those who stayed behind were just as concerned. They worried about the rescuers, the hostages, and the future of the clan.

Maddia surprised the group when she said, "The day could not be better. It is a good sign."

"But it is raining," said Lakus, her brother. "We shall be miserable."

"The rain means that the Lion People are not inclined to send out raiding parties today," said Maddia. "The mist will hide our movements."

"Maddia is right," added Lartha. The priestess went from person to person, touching each of them on the forehead as she did. She did the same with the two wolves, saying to them, "Take care of your humans. Bring them home unharmed."

The group set out without looking back. They knew that seeing their families would only make leaving more difficult. They stared down at the trail as they walked, and for now, they could think of nothing to say to one another.

Each of them carried some food, but not much. Because it was summer, they would be able to find fruit and edible plants. If they were lucky, they might hunt small animals or catch fish in the river, which they would follow most of the way. They had weapons and cutting tools. In addition, each of them had a length of vine. Carrying the vines was not easy, but they were not sure that the right kind of vine grew near the sea.

"As miserable as we are, the captives must have felt worse," commented Maddia. "They probably had no food. I wonder what they were thinking?"

"My guess is that they were thinking about only one thing," suggested Griffo. "How to stay alive."

"We will have much to discuss with them when they are free," said Tulio. He sounded as if he had no doubt that their plan would work.

They walked all day without resting. Each of them grabbed fruit as they went. Late in the afternoon, they found a place to stay the night. Not far from the river was an overhanging cliff. It gave them shelter from the rain and a place to light a fire safely. Even though it was summer, they would be more comfortable on a cool, wet evening with a fire. It would also keep animals away.

While Lakus and Piero made a fire, the others broke into two groups. One would hunt, and the other would try to catch fish in the river. Lakus and Piero found wood nearby that was more or less dry. Once the fire got started, even wet wood burned well. The hunters returned with a wild pig that the wolves had tracked down, but the fishermen were empty-handed.

"The river was high and muddy," said Fong apologetically. "But we picked fruit and some greens on the way back."

"That is not much of an excuse," teased Ganni, one of the hunters. "We had rain and mud, yet we got a wild pig."

"I think it is more precise to say that the wolves got the wild pig," said Zibio. The leader of the clan was pleased that the rescuers were able to joke with one another, even though the odds against them were terrible.

The wild pig, fruit, and vegetables made a fine meal that night. There were even leftovers for the next day. The rescuers slept well and continued the journey in the morning.

They made surprisingly good time over the next few days. The weather improved, and each night they found a sheltered place to sleep. None were as good as the cave of the first night, but they had few choices.

Their good luck almost came to an end on the

fourth day. At midday, as they were walking up a hill beside the river, they caught sight of a group of warriors from the Lion Clan. They were on a path that would bring them to the hill.

"This is something we do not need," said Zibio. "We cannot go forward or back, and we do not want to engage them."

Because of their position near the crest of the hill, the Wolf Clan could not be seen by the warriors. They had a little time to think about what to do, but not much. When the warriors came around the side of the hill, they would be able to see the rescuers.

"We can conceal ourselves individually," said Fong. "The complication will be regrouping and communicating that it is all clear."

"There is simply not enough vegetation here for us to hide as a group," said Griffo.

"We can try swimming across the river," said Maddia. "The current is slow here, and the river is not too wide. All of us have gone at least that distance during practice. If we swim in pairs, we will be able to assist one another if there is a need. We have to cross the river anyway."

No one spoke, but all of them looked at the river. The forest was thick on the other side, and they could hide from the Lion People.

"What if they see us?" asked Piero.

"That is a risk we have to take," answered Maddia. "We face the same problem here. They are far from the river, and the trail does not bring them any closer. Besides, if they looked in the river and saw us, they might not even understand what they saw. They would not be expecting to see humans swimming with wolves across the river."

"There is no time to discuss this any further," said Zibio. "We must cross the river, and we will be exposed whenever we do it. Now is the time."

"Remember, the flow of the water will be pulling us downriver. Try to stay together, but if we drift apart, come upriver and meet near that overhanging tree." Tulio pointed to a large tree that leaned over the water. It was one of the tallest trees in the forest and would be easy to see."

"I will go last with Nasha," suggested Maddia. "Tulio and Albo can go right before us. If the Lion People get here, we will have the wolves to help us, and we are the best swimmers." She added one more thing. "The vines will make it a little harder to swim, but they will help you float. Be patient, and do not panic."

Each of the adults paired with one of the young people, who were better swimmers. They slipped into the water and began paddling. As Tulio had said, the current caused them to drift downstream. All of them made it to the other side, as did Maddia, Tulio, and the wolves. The Lion People were not aware they had been there.

Once they had found one another, the rescuers went farther upriver. They were in the vicinity of the stronghold of the Lion People, so they had to stay in the forest between the river and the great sea. This made it more difficult to travel, but they did not want to risk being seen.

Vica recognized the hill they were looking for. She was more familiar with the territory and knew where to look. She pointed to the top of the hill, and they all understood. They reached the base of the hill at dusk. It was just a short distance to the shore of the sea, but because of the hill, they were hidden from view. They decided to stay there for the night.

"Before it gets dark, let us choose the trees we will cut," said Piero. "We can mark them with slashes so we know which ones are the right size. We can begin working at dawn."

The forest had many trees, and finding what they needed was easy. They even managed to cut a half dozen down before it became dark. They also realized that carrying the vines was a wise decision, even though swimming across the river with them had been tiring. No suitable vines grew in the area.

"Make a fire near those rocks," said Zibio, pointing at the base of the hill. "It cannot be too big, but we need it for protection. We will not be able to hunt tonight, so we will sleep with empty stomachs."

They slept fitfully, even though they were exhausted. Each noise woke them, as did concerns about the rescue attempt. As soon as the sky began to lighten in the morning, they got to work.

"Vica and I will catch some fish," said Lura. "She thinks there is a good spot nearby that is out of the sight of the Lion People."

Tulio kept a low fire going while Maddia and Piero gathered fruit. Nasha and Albo brought down a small goat. Maddia encouraged them to eat it themselves, knowing that the wolves had eaten less than the humans. When they returned to the fire, the fish were cooking, and they were able to put together a decent meal.

The rafts were completed by the middle of the afternoon. There was nothing else to do, so Zibio urged them to sleep. All of them needed it, and they dozed off immediately.

Maddia awoke to her father's voice, "We must be on our way," he said.

The sun was down, but the sky was still light. They brought the rafts to the shore of the sea. In addition to the rafts, they carried two long poles. With the poles, they would push against the bottom of the sea and move the rafts forward. Everything seemed ready.

Looking at the great sea for the first time, Piero was stunned by its size. Then he asked, "What if it gets too deep to use the poles?"

Because only a few of them had ever seen a body of water this vast, they had not considered what Piero said. They had only practiced in the stream and the river. His question took them completely by surprise.

"We can paddle with our hands," suggested

Maddia. "It is all we can do."

"That will never get us there," said Tulio. "There must be a better way."

Lura had motioned to Vica to explain the problem. Vica paced back and forth for a moment looking around. She saw a tree limb on the ground. With her sawing knife, she cut a piece from it that was as long as her leg. She knelt on the ground and looked at the others. She moved the stick beside her as if she were digging a hole.

"I know what she means," said Lura. "She thinks we can paddle with a stick in the same way that we make a hole with a digging stick."

"That will work," said Tulio. He pointed his finger at Vica, smiled, and nodded. She understood that he agreed with her, and she was pleased.

Working quickly, they all found sticks they could use as paddles. Fong complained that he could make better paddles if he had just a little more time, but that was not to be. They had to be on their way at once.

They slid the rafts into the water and climbed on board. The wolves wagged their tails, enjoying the adventure. The others had mixed emotions. They were excited to have attained this point in the rescue, but knew that the most difficult part lay before them.

Vica's idea proved to be necessary. They floated into deeper water sooner than any of them anticipated. The bottom of the sea dropped off quickly. The paddles worked, but not as well as they wanted. Each person paddled independently, and although the rafts moved forward, they did so clumsily.

"We can do better," said Tulio. "Think about when we moved the sun stones. We pulled the rope together at the same time. Try paddling together."

"Like we chant together," said Maddia.

Those in the raft with Maddia began to chant in low voices. They paddled in time with the chant, and the speed of the raft increased. The group in the other raft saw their friends and imitated them. The two rafts moved across the water together in the dim moonlight. Chanting lifted their spirits in an unexpected way and gave them a glimmer of hope in a seemingly impossible endeavor.

Chapter 22

The two rafts settled on the shore. Those on board stepped off carefully, making as little noise as they could. They lay down on the beach and crawled to the cover of the trees near the shore. The last person off each raft pulled it onto the beach. Working quietly, several of them carried the rafts into the brush and hid them.

Vica led the group with Griffo at her side. The moon cast a dim light, and they advanced from shadow to shadow. They were patient. One person at a time moved, and they stayed in the shadows whenever they could. Vica did not believe that many guards were patrolling at night, but they took no chances.

At the edge of the stronghold of the Lion People, they executed their plan. Vica and Griffo positioned themselves near the slave quarters. The others hurried past them following the base of the cliff. Their goal was to form a human chain so that the captives could see where they were supposed to go. Each person in the chain could see the next person. When the captives left the compound, they could move from person to person. If all went according to plan, the captives could escape into the forest beyond the stronghold. With darkness to shield them and a reasonable start, they would be deep in the forest before the Lion People grasped what happened.

Once everyone was in place, Griffo and Vica inched along the cliff. A guard was stationed in the narrow opening to the cave where the slaves lived. He was not sleeping, so their plan had to change. Vica decided that she had no choice but to approach the guard and strike him on the head with a short club. She signaled this to Griffo, who stood by if Vica needed him. Vica got to within a short distance of the guard before he turned and saw her.

Instead of shouting an alarm, he lunged toward her, grabbed her arms, and pushed her to the wall. With an evil grin, he growled, "Vica, I see you have returned. I heard that you and the girls had fled. Did you come back to see me?"

The guard put his forearm across her throat and continued pressing her against the wall. Griffo did not understand his words, but he knew what he had to do. He placed an arrow in his bow and took careful aim. The arrow struck the guard in the back, but it did not kill him. Vica pushed herself from the wall and knocked the guard over.

She jumped on top of him and put her hand over his mouth so he could not shout a warning. The guard struggled for a moment, but the fall backward had pushed the arrow into a vital organ and he died.

Griffo ran to the guard and dragged his body off while Vica slipped into the slave quarters. The first person she recognized was Murra. She woke her and put her finger in front of her mouth to show that she should be silent. When Murra saw Vica, she hugged her friend, realizing that their rescue was at hand. She watched Vica's gestures and saw Griffo in the dim moonlight at the mouth of the cave.

Vica and Murra woke the captives one by one. They understood at once what was happening and moved swiftly to Griffo and then out of the cave. More than a hundred captives were in the compound, and it took longer than they assumed to get them out. Vica and Griffo were anxious, but they knew that once the plan had been initiated, it could not be reversed. Fortunately, not a single captive chose to stay in the stronghold. All of them would rather have risked death than stay as prisoners of the Lion People.

Murra and her children reached Tulio and Albo. Murra thought that the wolf might frighten some of the captives from other clans and said to Tulio, "We will stay with you and Albo. The others will see he is harmless."

Tulio was about to object in order to protect

Murra and the children, but he realized that she was correct. Murra guided the others down the trail. The children hugged and petted Albo so the others could see he would not harm them.

The last captives to leave were Maril and Farad. They had helped the women with young children and were now scurrying toward the trail. Vica backed out to where Griffo was standing. They waited for a time to be sure none of the Lion People had been aroused. No one stirred in the center of the camp, so they withdrew to the position held by Tulio just outside the stronghold. They waited to give the captives time to move farther away.

The plan worked better than anyone had anticipated. All of the captives had gotten away, and none of the guards had been alerted. There was enough moonlight to let them see the path and proceed through the woods to safety. The Lion People would not awaken until dawn. All of this had been accomplished without a word being spoken by anyone.

At the moment when success seemed certain, a most unexpected thing happened. Nasha and Albo started to howl. It was a fearful sound, one that none of the clan had heard before. The wolves were afraid of something terrible.

"Stop them, Maddia," pleaded Zibio to his daughter.

"Nasha, Albo, come to me," whispered Maddia, but neither wolf moved toward her. They backed away from the cliff and sustained their howling.

At the same time, noises could be heard coming from the stronghold of the Lion People. The sounds seemed frightened, as if they expected an attack by wolves. The shouts quickly turned to rage as the Lion People saw that the captives were gone.

What had set the wolves off was something that the humans had not felt. The ground was shaking so slightly that they could not perceive it. The wolves, however, being more attuned to natural clues, knew at once that something was wrong.

"Please, Nasha," begged Maddia, almost in tears. "Please be quiet." She tried to put her arms around Nasha's neck to comfort her, but the wolf kept backing up, as did Albo.

In the distance, a group of the Lion People could be seen. They were on the path beside the cliff. They were waiting for their companions, and once a sufficient force had been gathered, they would go after the captives.

Nasha and Albo would not cease their howling and were pacing back and forth from the cliff to the treeless plain beside the sea. They acted as if they wanted the humans to accompany them, walking toward the group and then turning quickly. The plan, however, was to take flight through the forest. If the humans went toward the sea, the Lion People would discover them at once. The outcome would be terrible. The Lion People were well-armed and seasoned warriors, and only the rescuers had weapons. The captives would be defenseless. It is likely that all of them would die at the hands of the Lion People.

Like the others, Vica was on the verge of panic when she saw the wolves howl. Suddenly, she stopped moving. She knelt down on all fours for a moment, closed her eyes, and then jumped up. Her inability to hear caused her to pay more attention to her other senses, and she had felt the same vibration as the wolves. She did not know what was happening but was sure that something was wrong. She pointed at the wolves and ran toward them.

"Vica and the wolves are aware of something," said Maddia firmly. "We must trust them. Go where they lead us."

The wolves turned and ran to the flat spot beside the sea. Reluctantly, the rescuers and captives left the shelter of the trees. They were midway between the cliff and the sea when an earthquake struck. All of them were knocked to the ground by the temblor. Because nothing was around to come down on them, no one was seriously injured.

The Lion People were not so lucky. Their stronghold was beside a steep cliff, and many of them lived in caves in the cliff as well as in shelters beside it. The power of the earthquake caused the entire side of the mountain to give way. The chances of surviving the rockslide were slim.

The people of the Wolf Clan and the former captives watched with a mix of horror and relief at the destruction. They had never experienced an event like this. The ground shook again, but less severely. The worst of the earthquake was over, and they were uninjured.

Although he was as terrified as the others by what had happened, Zibio urged them to go on. "We cannot stay here a moment longer," he insisted. "We do not know how many of the Lion People survived, nor do we know the state of our village. The captives from other clans can come with us, or then can return to their own people."

Many of the captives were from local clans, and they chose to find their way home. Some of them would walk part of the way with the Wolf Clan. Others had no idea where they were. They decided to go with the rescuers. Among these were children who had lost their parents and had bonded with children and adults of the Wolf Clan.

"Zibio is right," said the boy Griffo, "but we should not follow our original route. We planned to stay in the narrow valleys. The shaking ground may have collapsed the walls of the valleys and blocked the trail. An even greater risk is that the ground will shake another time, and the walls will come down on us."

"We can follow the sea to the river," suggested Tulio. "It will not be far. We do not have to worry about the Lion People now, and there is nothing beside the sea or the river that can descend on us."

The group set off at once. They moved slowly because of the children, many of whom had to be carried. They pushed on through the night until the sun came up.

Maddia and a few others went ahead of the group to look for food. Because it was summer, the trees had fruit and berries. Some of the young people picked what they could, and others caught fish either with their hands or by spearing them. There was no time to make a fire and cook the fish, so they ate it raw. It was not a fine meal, but it would sustain them for the remainder of the day.

By sunset, they were worn out. Seeing a small grove of trees near the water, Zibio said, "We should not travel tonight. If we build a fire here, we will be safe when darkness comes. The trees will provide us with the wood we need for the fire. We can retreat to them if we are set upon." Even though he had seen the destruction of the Lion People's camp, he was still concerned.

Lakus and Maddia got wood while Tulio used his firestones to ignite some dry grass and kindling. It was not long before the fire was blazing, and for the first time since leaving the stronghold, the captives felt confident. No one was more pleased than the children. Some of them had been held by the Lion People for years.

All of the children were fascinated by Nasha and Albo. Encouraged by Maddia, they came to the wolves, which adored the affection they received. One after another, the children touched the wolves, and the bravest of them risked a hug. It was difficult for them to imagine that they were in the presence of one of the animals most feared by humans. Not only that, but the wolves had saved them.

Wearied by the events of the previous evening and long day, one by one, all of them dropped off to sleep except for the sentinels. Zibio, Vica, and some of the young men rotated as guards. Nasha and Albo dozed at the perimeter of the group, but they woke instantly at every sound. The night was uneventful, and they rose the next morning with renewed strength.

At daybreak, Vica and some of the women gathered fruit and berries. A group of men took the children to the water to catch more fish. Maddia and Lakus went hunting with the wolves and returned not long after with a small boar and some rabbits.

"Do we really want to waste time on cooking and celebrating now?" Ganni asked Zibio. The young man was clearly concerned about being pursued. Moreover, he was anxious to get to camp where his mother waited.

Zibio answered, "I share your apprehension, but I think we will make better progress if all of us are well-fed. Besides, for the captives, this is their first morning of freedom in a long time. Some of the children have not had a proper meal in years. Let them take pleasure in the moment."

Ganni could not help but to agree with Zibio.

The women who had been captive for so long were preparing the meal with a sense of contentment. The children were doing childish things: splashing in the water, playing with the wolves, and sneaking berries into their mouths before the meal.

After the morning meal, the group started off again. As Zibio predicted, they traveled quickly, and they encountered no threats for the rest of the journey. When they entered familiar territory, Tulio, Ganni, and Lakus were given permission to leave the group and run to the village. They wanted to inform the clan of the arrival of the captives and give them time to prepare a suitable celebration.

By the time the young people reached the village, they were ready to drop from fatigue. That did not keep them from delighting in a warm and enthusiastic reception. Preparations for a feast were begun, and some of the clan raced off to assist the rescuers and the rescued. They realized that the trek had been demanding on all of them, especially the young children.

When the remainder of the group arrived, the reunion was magnificent. People came together as never before, and the members of the other clans were treated with sincere friendship. The bonds that had grown among the captives during their imprisonment were extended to their families. The outsiders were welcomed so graciously that they were brought to tears. The captives who thought they had lost everything—their homes, their friends, and their family—now had a second chance at a decent life.

Chapter 23

It took several days for the people of the Wolf Clan to resume their normal routine. They felt sorrow about those who had perished because of the Lion People, but they believed that the spirits of those who had passed on would have a new life. The survivors were soon caught up with everyday chores, the most essential being finding food. Because it was midsummer, fruit and vegetables were easy to find. In addition to feeding the clan now, as much as possible would be put away for the winter.

As Maddia and her friends were returning from a hunt, she looked toward the hill where the sun stones has been raised. She turned to her brother Tulio and said, "We never finished. There is one more stone to raise."

Tulio did not answer at once. He had been thinking the same thing, but was uncomfortable discussing it. "I did not want to say anything about the stones. It might seem as if I was doing it for myself."

"You were never doing it for yourself," answered Maddia. "You suggested raising the stones to honor the sun. We have even more reason to do it now. The sun stones will help us remember those who fell trying to save us."

No one said a word after Maddia spoke, but they all felt as she did. When the group arrived back at camp, they went to Lartha's hut. Maddia asked the priestess about raising the final stone, knowing that her brother was still reluctant to speak.

"I agree with you," said Lartha. "The longest day will soon arrive. Perhaps raising the final stone will be what all of us need to put the events of the recent past behind us. I shall discuss the matter with Zibio."

The new leader of the clan saw the wisdom of completing the job and raising the final sunstone. The next day, they returned to the ridge with a renewed sense of purpose.

Before the final stone could be placed, Lartha had to determine its location. The crowd moved to the side of the dolmen to give the priestess a clear view of the opening and the stakes in the ground that showed where on the horizon the sun would set on the longest day. Maddia stood not far away. Nasha and Albo were curled up on the ground just beyond her. As Maddia walked down the slope to the wolves, she noticed something unusual. She looked again to be sure her conclusion was correct and approached Lartha.

"I am sorry to interrupt you, Lartha," said Maddia quietly, "but there is something you should see." Even though Maddia had known Lartha all of her life and worked with her often, she was not comfortable disturbing Lartha in a situation like this.

"What is it, Maddia?" said the healer as she walked toward the girl.

While the others wondered what was going on, the girl brought Lartha to where the wolves were lying. She faced the summer stones and said, "On the longest day, the sun will set behind the hill with the round top. It will shine through the standing stones in this direction." Turning somewhat, she pointed at the three winter stones. "On the shortest day, the sun will set behind the mountain with three peaks. The rays of the sun on both days will come through the standing stones to this spot."

The place where Maddia was standing sloped upward to the sun stones on the crest of the ridge. The angle of the slope meant that just before setting, the sun's rays would shine through the standing stones to this point on both the longest and shortest days.

"You have made a wonderful observation," responded Lartha. "What caused you to think of it?"

"When I came over to Nasha and Albo, I saw

where you were standing in line with the sun. I looked at the winter stones and saw the same alignment. I did not really think of anything. I just found myself here."

Glancing at the two wolves lying on the ground, Lartha added, "Perhaps the wolves being here was not an accident. In any case, you have chanced upon something of importance that we should discuss with the others. Ask them to come over here with us."

Maddia brought the rest of the group to where Lartha was standing. The priestess explained the significance of the point, crediting Maddia and the wolves with the discovery. When they heard Lartha's explanation, the other clan members turned and looked at both the winter and summer stones. They experienced an unusual sensation and recognized its importance. To these people, the place where the sun's rays shone on the two most important days was indeed magical.

"Should we not raise a stone here, too?" asked Griffo, and the others echoed his question.

Lartha looked down at the ground and then at the sun stones. "Let me think about it. This is a good time for all of you to rest and take food."

With that, Lartha walked toward the sun stones. While the others ate, she sat between the sun stones and stared at the horizon. Those who were familiar with her suspected that she had entered a trance state, something she often did when there was an important matter to consider.

Although some of her trances lasted for much of the day or night, this one did not. Within a short time, she rose and came to the group carrying small rocks.

"What I am about to tell you will be surprising. Instead of raising a stone, I think we should consider moving one of the winter stones and placing it in the ground here." She put her rocks on the ground. "The stone has already been touched by the winter sun on the shortest day, so it is only fitting that it meet the summer sun."

At first, silence greeted Lartha's suggestion. Then a voice said, "Can we move it now?" It was Piero, the brother of Ganni.

Lartha's smile was enough of an answer for the others to cheer, and immediately they ran toward the winter stones. Nasha and Albo joined in the fun, often nipping playfully at the human members of their pack. Fong was about to say that it would make more sense for some of them to stay and dig the hole, but he decided not to dampen their enthusiasm. He walked to the stone with Tulio and Lartha, and the three of them planned how they would proceed.

"We can make this a simple task," said Fong when they arrived. "Because there is a downhill slope, the stone will probably move itself. We have to lower it carefully onto the rolling logs and be sure they do not move until we are ready. We will also have to secure the stone with ropes."

"How will we get the stone out of the hole?"

asked Maddia.

"We hope that will be easy," answered Tulio. "Come and help me," he said and looked at Lakus and Griffo.

The three strong boys put their weight on the sun stone and moved it just a bit. They went to the other side and did the same. Understanding what they were doing, others got on the opposite side of the stone. The two groups took turns pushing, and it was not long before the stone was loose in the ground.

Fong and Tulio tied rope to the stone and had a number of the stronger men hold it. Vica and Lura each prepared to put a wooden post on the side of the stone that was leaning toward the ground. The four boys pushed the stone just a little. When they did, Vica and Lura moved the posts into position. The men holding the ropes let the stone rest on the posts. After repeating this several times, the stone rested at a sharp angle on the posts.

"Stack some of the squared logs under the stone," said Fong. "They will keep the stone from falling. Put them close to the middle of the stone."

When the logs were in place, Vica and Lura pulled their posts away slowly so the stone would not crash onto the logs. They slid the bottom of the posts along the ground until the stone rested on the logs.

Now Fong and Tulio did something that seemed amazing to those who saw it. They pushed down gently on the end of the stone until it was on top of a rolling log. Fong held it in this position, and Tulio went around to the other side. With gentle nudges, Fong slid it forward, and the stone moved onto the rolling log. Because so much of the weight of the stone rested on the rolling log, Fong could remove one of the flat-sided logs. With another push, it slid onto two rolling logs.

"Tie the rope to the stone again," said Fong, "and hand me one of the posts, Lura."

Fong put the end of the post on the ground, held the top, and pushed the middle against the stone. This kept it from sliding down the hill while the ropes were being attached. Once they were, and some of the men held the ropes, he let the stone move. He asked Tulio to get the other post. They took turns letting the stone drift down the hill. Using the posts and the ropes, they controlled the movement of the stone easily and moved it to the spot that Lartha had marked.

Digging the hole took less time than anyone expected because everyone wanted to be involved. They used spears and hand tools, being careful to put the dirt on the side of the hole that was away from the stone. When it was deep enough, the stone was rolled on the logs until it slid into the hole. Pulling on the ropes and pushing with posts brought the stone into the vertical position. Dirt and small rocks were packed around the stone, and the job was done.

Before returning to the camp, Tulio looked back at what they had accomplished. He asked no one in particular, "I wonder if anyone will remember we did this?"

On the longest day, the Wolf Clan and several other tribes gathered at the sun stones. Word had spread about the dolmen and the stone that would be touched by both the winter and summer stones. The people who stood near the stones were amazed at what they saw. When the rays of the sun passed through the dolmen and touched the center stone, they were breathless.

As the sun set, Lartha said in a voice that all could hear, "With these stones, we honor both the sun and those who gave their lives for us. Let us never forget them. Their spirits are welcome here."

Among those who visited the sun stones on that special day was Valtar's clan. The leader was with his wife, Maril, and their son, Farad. They spent time with Ducatha, Murra, and the other captives. The bond between the clans, which had already been good, had been strengthened even more.

Years later, Farad would take as his wife the girl Salora he had met when she was a prisoner of the Lion People. The two of them, others from both clans, and some of Nasha's pups would leave and head west. They had heard that the animals were plentiful in that direction, and that the plants produced abundant fruit.

The stories proved to be true, and the move was successful. The group thrived, and during the succeeding generations, their descendents continued moving west. They brought with them the family story of the day that the rays of the sun passed through the dolmen. To commemorate the memory of their ancestors and to thank the sun for its warmth and light, they built stone monuments of their own.

Many years passed, and the humans reached the far western sea. They crossed a finger of land to a beautiful place that would become an island as the glaciers melted and the seas rose. The story of the standing stones came with them. In time, these humans built their own monument. Their circle of great stones would stand forever as a symbol of human achievement and a tribute to those who had passed on to the spirit world.